SAUCERS FIRST CONTACTED REVEALED
20Th Century Times

Orfeo Angelucci

SAUCERIAN PUBLISHER
Original Sources in Ufology

ISBN: 978-1-955087-40-7

9 781955 087407

2022, Saucerian Publisher

Orfeo Angelucci (1912-1993)

INTRODUCTION

Throughout human history, people have seen things they can't explain. In antiquity, people referred to them as angels, demons, deities, or whatever. That changes with the scientific revolution, where people wonder if the points of light they see are alien. However, World War II marked the beginning of a new phase of interest. During this conflict, Allied pilots flying at night over German reported seeing balls of light following their aircraft. Nicknamed "foo fighters," these ghostly flyers were said to be one of Germany's secret weapons.

Kenneth Arnold's historic 1947 sighting–combined with a highly publicized UFO incident that occurred later that summer near Roswell, New Mexico, fueled the public interest in otherworldly visitors. It established an entire new field known as "ufology."

On June 24, 1947, media across the country reported that a civilian pilot named Ken Arnold spotted bright objects streaking across the sky at supersonic speeds near Mount Rainier in Washington. We will never know what private pilot Kenneth A. Arnold saw 75 years ago while flying past Mt. Rainier on June 24, 1947. What he said he saw, and spent the rest of his life trying to explain, added the words "flying saucer" to the vocabularies of millions of people worldwide. The event that we know today as the "first modern era of UFO sightings" gave birth to the contemporary movement of UFOs.

Most of us go on about our lives, enjoying the predictable routine of family, work, and, if we're lucky, a little bit of leisure. But if you're Orfeo Angelucci – aerospace worker, family man, thoughtful but average citizen, one day you get contacted by a race of advanced, extraterrestrial beings that reveal to you the secret of the universe, your purpose here, and the task ahead that would change his life forever.This was the incredible claim in Angelucci's book, The Secret of the Saucers, which tells the story of his contact with a pair of kind, ethereal entities who want him to share their message of peace and love for the human race. But these warm greetings came with a warning: that we must change our harmful ways or suffer the fate of the world that came before us.

Orfeo Matthew Angelucci (Orville Angelucci) (June 25, 1912 – July 24, 1993) was one of the most unusual of the mid-1950s so-called "contactees" who claimed to be in contact with extraterrestrials.Angelucci claimed that he suffered from poor health and extreme nervousness for most of his life and eventually moved for health-related reasons from Trenton, New Jersey, to California in 1948, where he took a job on the assembly line at the Lockheed aircraft plant in Burbank. Another contactee, George Van Tassel, was also employed for a time at this plant.

In his books, Orfeo Angelucci says he was particularly terrified of thunderstorms and was attracted to California because he had heard that thunderstorms were very rare there. Angelucci wrote the first version of his theories of matter, energy and life, *The Nature of Infinite Entities* in 1952, based on "research" done earlier in Trenton, including launching a giant cluster of weather balloons.

Beginning in the summer 1952, according to Angelucci in his book *The Secret of the Saucers* (1955), he began to encounter flying saucers and their friendly human-appearing pilots during his drives home from the aircraft plant. These superhuman space people were handsome, often transparent, and highly spiritual. Eventually, Angelucci was taken in an unmanned saucer to earth orbit, where he saw a giant "mother ship" drift past a porthole. He also described having experienced a "missing time" episode. Eventually, he remembered living for a week in the body of "space brother" Neptune, in a more evolved society on "the largest asteroid", the remains of a destroyed planet, while his usual body wandered around the aircraft plant in a daze.

In his later book, The Son of the Sun, Angelucci related an account that he claimed had been told to him by a medical doctor calling himself Adam, whose experiences were similar to his own. He also published several pamphlets on space-brotherly themes, such as "Million Year Prophecy" (1959), "Concrete Evidence" (1959), and "Again We Exist" (1960).

This title is an authentic reproduction of the original Angelucci's February, 1953 newspaper printed text in shades of gray. **IMPORTANT**, even though we have attempted to maintain the integrity of the original work, the present reproduction can have missing letters and, blurred pages, poor pictures from the original scanned copy. Some of the original pages are shadowy and faint. This title has been formatted from their original broadsheet format version to a traditional letter size for publication.

Great, but unpretentious, this title is an extraordinarily rare symbol of what was going on in those early years of the modern UFO phenomena.

Editor
Saucerian Publisher, 2022

EXTRA | 20th Century Times

Vol. 1, No. 1   2931 Glendale Blvd., Los Angeles 39, Calif.   25c Per Copy

SAUCERS FIRST CONTACT REVEALED

Avalanche In The Skies

The "flying saucers" invaded our skies, writing incredible history in the archives of man. Five years of amazing capers were brought to a spectacular climax in the summer of 1952. Particularly during the last two weeks of August.

Large numbers of people became enthusiastic with expectations of probable mass landings by them. Many became permanently convinced that the earth was finally to be "invaded" by an intelligent civilization, one of many in the countless other worlds. There remains a brand of thinkers who will not give up the "ghost," and having to some extent deciphered "the writing in the sky", these expect to see periodic reappearances.

They will not be disappointed. Indeed, not only will they come to life again, but they will become more and more manifest of reality with each cycle. Perhaps, the year 1953 will be the time when they will not only be seen, but also heard.

They Are Friends

saucers," yet never did they pose or expose themselves to cameras, telescopes, radar, pursuit planes, or any other agency, in such a manner, or long enough that their secrets could be recorded, deciphered, and exploited. In their hands we are as soft putty.

The avalanche of 1952 had definite pattern and purpose. We cannot grasp the full picture if we continue to call them flying saucers, for the term misleads us from their reality and their character. The material composing them is basically a plastic-suspended crystal, with functioning essentials. Therefore it would be appropriate to call their ships CRYSTAL SHIPS; and the "flying saucers" what they are, CRYSTAL DISCS. By these terms we will realistically understand them.

We Are Surveyed

The crystal discs made their most vivid appearances near and around definite places of interest, such as atomic research centers, armed forces installations, Washington, D.C., and others. This is a significant writing in the sky,

They Are Friends

Not only have we been long under intelligent observation, but we are in their power and control. However, there is nothing to fear. They cannot harm us; no more than the sun could. One reason is that they would not under almost any circumstance. The other is the mysterious inviolable codes of nature which actively rebukes any excesses which oppose its immu-■■■ irreversible courses. Nothing can stop the earth from its onward evolution to a state of virtual perfection.

The Space Visitors are friends. The author will stand up for this to any limit, for I know one who has stepped from one of the crafts. For a brief time this one contact, (one of us), had become as one of the visitors in a transcendant sense. He literally exisited "b e t w e e n two worlds".

Since Kenneth Arnold first reported his sighting near Mount Ranier modern civilization has become alerted and conscious to the realities of space travel already achieved by others. Arnold's sighting is dated as June 24, 1947.

Coral Lorenzen, of Sturgeon Bay, Wisconsin, claims to have sighted one while living in Doug-las Arizona. She felt sure that she

a significant writing in the sky, so apparent that even the skeptics had to recognize it. But was there any result, or effect from any of their behaviors? Let us see.

They brought the thinking of officials and personnel of our entire armed forcves to realize that our aircraft and facilities are rapidly becoming obsolete, and very clumsy. We are rowing up the wrong way. The "flying saucers" actually prevented the free world from a swift and utter defeat, impending because of some secret strategies of "an enemy." (Details are classified information, in our interest.) For science, they are a first clue that universal forces exist which we have not yet been aware of, or tapped.

We were re-surveyed in the avalanche of 1952. Every man, woman and child is recorded in vital statistics by our visitors. Every point of progress of our society is registered with them. They know us as we do not know ourselves. In us they again see their own world going through the "growing pains," which it experienced in its history. And, it is beyond them to interfere even if they could. Yet a contact with even one earth being were permissible, if accomplished in the proper order—unviolating—effective—retractible.

sighted one while living in Douglas, Arizona. She felt sure that she had witnessed a space ship, even though talk of such was limited to science fantasy. But this was 1947, and few people could perceive an epic emerging, as one had just died with World War II.

But Kenneth Arnold and Coral Lorenzen, even in that embryonic period, were so impressed that they have not ceased to be active in the subject. They had observed a wonder, not a mirage.

Thousands of reports followed. Large numbers seemed to come in definite, periodic cycles. As in everything else, the excitement gave birth to hoaxes, and some peculiar rantings of cranks. But those who even once had sighted a flying disc could not be perturbed. They will never be moved by cynics, or fooled by hoaxers.

The very name they have inherited, "flying saucers" makes them a natural target for comedy . . . as it was meant to be. For our own stability, the visitors ordain that we receive them lightly at first. We must mature to the impact of the meeting of worlds in the near future. Time means less than the occasion to an intelligence such as theirs.

Objects Are Crystaloid in Structure

Thousands have seen "flying proper order—unviolating—effective—retractible.

They must not interfere beyond merely turning a grain of dust, the feeling of one hair, and thereby remove a snag from the forward flow of destiny; one subtle contact, itself meshed into the cosmic motion of the universe. Beyond that, the questions are not answered, to them nor by them.

Oddly enough, Europeans, and more so the British have a more serious attitude toward the flying discs, even if static. Yet it is the Americans who have been intensively aroused.

Their active patterns pointed subtley to the realistic if we would but heed the signs. As sequences of time, well synchronized, they made their appearances over nations that in event of a global war would be our bulwarks, our tough lines of defense. The line between a civilized future and its alternative—abysmal slavery.

These nations were Swenden, Portugal, Greece, Turkey, Egypt, England, Italy, Australia, Japan, and some in South America. But who could discern such indirect allusions? Who will even seriously admit them?

The magnitude of events in our times staggers the inmagination and credulence of any mortalAnd now these things?

WELCOME SPACE VISITORS

The "flying saucers" are surely the greatest mystery in all history so far as active events, and visual manifestations are concerned. Thinking mankind gropes for an explanation of them. If they never occur again, then what indeed was their nature? If they recurr and stay in our skies who could ignore them?

One thing has been demonstrated. When they occur they are seen and reported. When they do not occur they are not seen nor reported. That is settled.

And now this narrative appears among us. There can only be one of two conclusions for it. It is either a yarn or real. If it is a yarn, it is one of the strangest in our annals. If it is true, then what?

No matter what it is, it takes us into an infinity of space, and into an infinite degree of self-examination. Therefore it is in one way or the other as real as life, as moving as motion, as true as the universe.

It cannot merely be read and thrust side. It demands to be read again, and again. Penetrate the inferrences, the galaxy of meanings in all its simplicity. Slowly but surely one can feel one's self unfolding, evolving into a new being from inherent potentials. If it is resisted, then one needs more self examination by meditation.

It promises a meeting of our world with another. The sooner we progress to the stature required for such an event, the sooner this meeting would come about. It is up to Earth to mature by natural courses. It is up to the "Other World" to decide the appointment.

It seems that we have everything to gain; nothing to lose.

The Editor

But let us pause. Can anyone imagine the future in the absence of these revelations? Where are we going? Is utter materialism to be our desolate end? Indeed it would be in the direction we were going. Nourishment for the spirit was all but exhausted. Science, on the other hand, is lumbering along with little to be added fundamentally. A truly global war looms in the dark horizon. Were we of the free world able to meet the challenge

We were approaching a dead end. But the 'flying saucers" could not see it that way. In return we should institute "Space Visitors Day." Once each year we could dedicate ourselves to the greatest of all realities. the greatest hope on mortal basis.

Their Search for a Contact

Did our space visitors execute any contact privious to, and during their 1952 survey? Thousands of people believe so.

Their conviction is that somehow, somewhere, a human being was materially contacted. But even the most avid fanatic recoils in disbelief when it is asserted positively that a contact was made. Especially when the incident is far removed from the conception that most people would have of such an incredible possibility. Almost every one seems to have either a preposterous picture in mind, or one in the terms of a "hot rod" curi-

ion, perhaps, but one very hard to change. Yet this very vision would limit the talents of the great Creator to a mere speck in the universe. would it not? That is settled. Our minds are primitive as yet. We believe the impossible, and spurn the inevitable truths; or we "swallow a camel, and strain at a gnat." Yet when some have been told that we are no wise ready for a mass meeting between worlds, they have indignantly raised their opposite opinions, as though their intelligence were insulted. It is merely further proof of our stature at present.

Our space visitors see us as we are, even if we cannot. Therefore, their search for a contact was difficult, and required a precision that is hard for us to comprehend. To them it was one of their most important and interesting phases of their observations.

The time had arrived. Who would be their "victim?" In the presence of human weakness and clumsiness it would need be one powerless to make any trouble, regardless of his own temptations. Yet he must be one to take the impact on the nervous system, and assure the success of the gentle event. He must be one who could assume the cosmic magnitude of the revelations, yet a mere spark, which would surely and slowly blazon into an aurora. The subject would need

the terms of a "hot rod" curiosity in the people from a neighbor world. If anyone has a rational conception of such a divine incident, they have failed to come forward. The gadget and fiction conception must be forgotten. Leave that for the little tots of marbles and dolls.

———

The contact was sure to be executed. The very time tables of destiny demanded it. It was to be of specific qualifications, which would satisfy nature and the high intelligence of other beings. The precision of the phenomenon was entirely out of the scope of the earth, and completely in the hands of . . . Of whom? Did the earth not matter? To we living here it was the only thing that mattered. We and its history were the only vibrant life. A narrow vis-aurora. The subject would need have some understanding of things in a cosmological order, and the relation of one thing to another.

If they wanted to make material landings on a grand scale the event would ocur beyond any shadow of a doubt; an event that would bring leaders of science, government and theology to embrace them. That is our way. It is not theirs.

Back to 1941. World War II was of little interest to them. What they sought for were signs that would reveal certain types of people. Their attention was focused on scientists, airplane pilots, special activities, and the public in general, that some response might come forth.

In 1947 the search had narrowed to three possible subjects. These were one in India, one in

Rome, one in New Jersey. Three unknowns. The choice was to be made from one of these.

Two thouand miles from the earth a huge mother space ship hovered. In this benevolent ship the screening had been completed. The choice was decided on the one in New Jersey. The search ended at a small farm on Kuser Road near Trenton, five acres called Albor.

The Contact

An experiment was being conducted on the little farm on Kuser Road. Some common mold was being sent into the high atmosphere suspended from 18 navy type balloons, under the direction of one, Orfeo. It was a peculiar investigation. Only he knew what he was trying to determine in this hardly professional and technical test. The date is August 4, 1946. The others in the group included two newspaper photographer-reporters, his father-in-law, two friends, some of the neighbors looking on, and some young boys.

Orfeo was a fundamentalist in general. For him all effects must have causes, and the desire to know the fundamentals of things was deeply ingrained. He was dubbed everything from scatter-brain to mad scientist, because of his seeming restless nature, ever jumping from one subject to another. Yet, this was not pure instability, but rather a mobile attention focused here and there wherever clues or signs pointed to possible causes or reasons. To give one example. For a short time he centered his attention on the crowing of a rooster, and from a few observations concluded that the rooster was made to crow for the stability of the sensitive nervous system of the hens, whose nervous system is in a way similar to the human nervous system. Thus, to him the "range Paralysis" of these fowl was precisely the "polio" in the human host.

This day, this ascension of balloons, the entire idea was merely another one of his efforts to satisfy "curiosity." In the skies something was hovering, something that intercepted the balloons, and in some very mysterious manner data was "exchanged" between these inert things. Another world was observing. But this was the last thing in the minds of any of the group launching the balloons. Why the interest centered here, and why it evolved into one of the most incredible events on the human scene is a conjecture whose answer in full rests only with the "visitors" from another world.

Why would a high intelligent people from another world be concerned about such a nondescript "hobby" from an apparent dreamer who knew not what he was doing? There were thousands of serious, stable, well learned people on earth, who were practical. Yet this slender ghost of a man attracted more and more their attention.

Let us review the facts briefly, and get behind the scenes.

In 1929 Orfeo was forced to leave school, not even passing the ninth grade. His health, a nervous condition, would not permit him to continue. He did very little work on any of the subjects, except typewriting and — science. Science remained rooted within him, and he excelled in its first high school year.

From then on he went to work as estimator-salesman, on the road for his people's flooring and stucco concern. True, he attempted many times to continue learning. in night school, but his "nerves" made the effort impossible. He was a victim of "constitutional inadequacy," subject to terrible migraine headaches, and extreme lassitude from any physical effort.

Thus he floundered from 1930 to 1937, devoted to his work, yet each day obsessed with the fundamentals of physics, from the nucleus of the hydrogen atom to the limitless bounderies of the universe. His health went from bad to worse. Finally even his interest in scientific things faded and all but left him.

In 1936 he was married. Five months later, from a clear sky he suffered the first onslought of a breakdown, a nervous condition labelled Neuro-Vascular Disturbance. It is much worse than it sounds, effecting the motor and autonomic nervous system, and the blood vessels and capellaries. No physical or mental suffering could be worse.

Fortunately, his father and two uncles doted on him even to their own sacrifice. Orfeo made an effort to deserve this good fortune, which he knew was not the lot of all those in such straits.

His weight had rapidly dropped from about 150 to 103 pounds. This was not a happy plight for a young man who loved to swim, the outdoors, to ramble through a woods, and to associate with people; who breathed-in a calm, sunny day, or thrilled to a storm at the shore.

of these "escapes," he drove his car to the front of his apartment. His mother was waiting for him with her head in the open window. As he came out of the car he heard her ask, weepingly:

"Do you come from Frank's house?"

He replied that he had not stopped there at all.

'Frank is dead. He took his own life with a revolver."

Orfeo was now ashamed of himsel... ing fled like a senseless person in a mere thunderstorm, while his beloved friend blasted himself into eternity. But his condition would tolerate no extreme emotion, and he remained somewhat poised. He had long ago learned to smile even when a knife twisted in his own heart.

Reality Is Burned

The next day Peter, brother of the departed Frank, came to Orfeo's house, driven there by another. In the car was the mattress soaked with a large cloud of blood. Peter asked that it be burned in the presence of the two only, he and Orfeo. Thus they stood watch, and talked as the flames consumed the memory. To Orfeo the fire seemed to be devouring away genius, reality, loyalty, fundamentals. Tonight he would see Frank; talk to him, find consolation in him. But Frank was gone with the last embers of that fire. Peter and he talked on for some time.

Orfeo, never quite well again from his condition, was now in

It became a different world, one spent among many doctors, some hospitals, and from the bed to the couch for 18 long months. Science and fundamentals were dead for him. His new interest became of a social strata, to help make a world which the meek, the suffering, and children would find more to their tolerance. Perhaps it was a dream. The New York World's Fair was already underway in plans, and though he never hoped to live to its day he did hope it would launch the new era.

Meantime he had met a brilliant young man. ~~Frank~~ was virtually a genius for his 22 years. Frank worked during the day, supporting his young brothers and sister, and was enrolled in the night class of the Rutgers University bacteriology course. He and Orfeo became at once fast friends, but in tantalizingly different aspects. Frank remained the unmovable realist, while Orfeo was now a hopeless idealist. But Frank put his all in every endeavor that Orfeo put into action, and became a supporting pillar to him.

Together they conceived and materialized such promotions as the "First Trenton Mardival," a preview of New Jersey beach resort seasons; the "Pan-American Exhibit," which became the World's Industrial Fair on the Million Dollar Pier in Atlantic City; the Pan-American move-

a vaccuous state of existence. He longed to know real health, but it seemed to be a longing never to be fulfilled. To add to the suffering, many doctors, and people in general labelled nervous troubles as figments of faulty thinking, and faulty attitudes, which could be easily overcome "if one tried." Man's inhumanity to man. But that was the pattern of general thought, and psychiatrists were perpetually aggravating the situation. However, most of the general practitioners were sincere and called a spade a spade. Orfeo's condition was ser~~ious and hopeless, yet not neces~~sarily dangerous to life itself.

With Frank's demise Orfeo had lost interest even in promotions which had been filling his enthusiasm. His life seemed to be pointless. Besides he was bearing physical tortures which no doctor understood, and no book evaluated.

—————

Somehow, somewhere, sometime, the fact that science was rearing its head behind all human events penetrated Orfeo's consciousness again. Theories and mechanics were being sharpened by technology. The whole world was in unrest. Hitler and Mussolini were stirring up hurricanes of humanity, refusing to let the world slumber on. To Orfeo, the sense that a demanding situation pervaded the world fundamentals, reasons, science,

City; the Pan-American movement, to foster cooperative relationships between the two great Americas. All these hatched and energized within one year. Dreams, dreams, and more dreams.

Finally, Frank, the realist, asked Orfeo to give up the ghost. For others made profits on his dreams, and he himself never made one penny from them. Could he not see the futility of it all?

Orfeo could not see a futility. He had at the same time gone back to the road for his people's concern, but his ideals continued to haunt him and to be another half of his existence.

———

Orfeo was controlled by a horrible phobia of lightning. When a thunderstorm loomed he became panicky, and would run or drive anywhere at all. Anywhere "but here" seemed to be his motive. If a storm came up in the middle of the night he would rise, half-dressed rush to the car and race away, preferably to town in some tall building. No other danger in the mad rush mattered. His capers had become an accepted thing by all who knew him. His phobia was indeed a hopeless case.

One night, returning from one

fundamentals, reasons, science, disease and health—all began to take deep hold. Now he yearned for Frank. But Frank was gone, and he had to support the interests once more alive in him alone, with no help from his friend's capabilities.

Rapidly his insatiable thirst for understanding the very nature of the atom, the cause of virus ailments, the mechanism of the entire universe must need be answered satisfactorily. Where was the cube root of all things? For indeed all things resolve finally into a complete oneness. The creation of matter—or the origin of the atom was the answer.

Ah, yes. His acute phobia of lightning had made of him quite an expert on the mechanism of atmospheric static electric, and there were mysterious characteristics about it that were not in the books, nor at the comprehension of experts in the field. He observed its patterns, by the most scatterbrain process one can imagine. He noticed that chickens were frightened by rain— but it was a particular type of rain. Chickens are apprehensive during an impending thunderstorm. Why? Unrelated questions here and there disclosed to him that chickens are subject to a "range paralysis." Every aspect of it parallels infantile paralysis in human beings.

In time he was to write to the White House, hoping to get a letter from the then President Franklin D. Roosevelt. It was hard to believe, but the President had prepared the way for him to be heard by Dr. John L. Lavan Jr., director of research at the time. If Dr. Lavan was convinced on Orfeo's conceptions and plans is hard to say. But he did refer him to Dr. Joseph Stokes of Children's Hospital in Philadelphia, who was working along the vitamin therapy.

Orfeo never went there, for it was a work opposing his theories; that some vitamin, of the B complex, was largely responsible for the nutrition of the virus. (This has been entirely substantiated.)

In certain types of atmospheric conditions he learned that wild mushrooms also "suddenly grew up." The fungus world became his target. In time he decided that mold was a form of negative life leaching on living matter, in subtle cases by the very process of mutation, a process illusive indeed, even to the best trained minds.

An "Airplane" Observes Them

It was impossible for a modern laboratory to employ him. He had to conduct any observation, test or study by himself, at his own time and expense. We were ing was heard of them again.

Orfeo reflected. How fine our airplanes had been developed, so soon after the war. There was a truly expert and mature pilot. To think that such a one, and such a craft had been attracted with keen interest to his little project. Little did he know—nothing was in the minds of people as "flying saucers." This was the contact. And for 5 years and 9 months he remained under constant observation by beings from another world, never aware of it, himself. At the end of that time it was to develop into one of the most incredible events in human history.

Various times Orfeo had gone to the Palmer Physics Laboratory of the Princeton University to discuss some fundamental problems and phenomenon on cosmic rays and atomics. Dr. Dan Davis, head of the Cosmic Ray department always found time to talk with him.

Two days after the balloons had been released and lost he again stopped in at the laboratory and recounted the events to Dr. Davis and one of his aids. Dr. Davis asked Orfeo why he did not let him know in advance. The laboratory would be glad to supply the hydrogen gas to him at cost, and reduce his expense. Also he would have arranged for the balloons to be followed by radar by the chain of stations in the entire eastern section.

now well into the war, and Penicillin had made its debut with mankind. But it was yet a not well-understood subject, and no books or reports were available. It was still a deep mystery to the public.

However, Orfeo was already well under way in finding out on his own the characteristics of the fungi. He was able to see that one of the most common molds could be made to produce chemicals indefinitely if kept in proper nutrition and temperatures. Then he decided to see what structural changes would occur in the upper atmosphere to the mold Aspergillus Clavatus in any of three stages: the embryonic period, the half-mature stage, and the mature.

It was now 1946, and the war had ended, the atom had been definitely split asunder. Penicillin was now widely known. Marvels at every turn. Yet too slow, too creeping, in this restless mind. Always the questions, what; why; how; prodded.

August 4th, the cultures were ready to be sent aloft by balloons. The sky was blue, the weather ideal. The cultures had been prepared every day by sets, so that the proper timings would be on hand for such a day.

Eighteen navy type balloons, strong in tandem lifted off the basket containing the molds. By some mishap the entire arrangement broke away prematurely.

Radar? . . . What would have been seen besides the balloons? Was it time for such a revelation? There are no answers as yet to such questions.

Princeton and its environs were a heaven to a science addict. In the vicinity were such institutions as Rockefeller Institute for Medical Research; the R.C.A. Laboratories; American Telephone and Telegraph Company; Institute for Advance Study; Heyden Chemical Corporation, producers of Penecillin. And nearby such as Rutgers University, E. R. Squibb & Son, Merck & Co., and many others.

Not too far off was the Evans Laboratory, where the first Radar contact was made with Earth's satellite, the Moon. This was in another era the laboratory of Marconi. From border to border Orfeo loved New Jersey, every inch of it. All but the thunderstorm. No greater geographical love did he have, nor greater phenomenal fear.

In November, 1947, Orfeo and his family started off for Los Angeles, by way of the Mayo Clinic at Rochester, Minnesota, here to keep an appointment with Dr. Walter C. Alvarez, the modern Hippocrates of diagnostics. Many of the mightiest would give half their fortunes for merely an appointment with this giant of medicine, who remained extremely modest in the peak of greatness.

The whole thing was lost as the mass rose higher and higher into the clear blue. It presented an attractive sight, nevertheless, and those present watched on for quite a while, as the spectacle became smaller and smaller.

Suddenly, and seemingly from nowhere, an airplane must have been attracted to the ascending cluster. It hovered and circled around them. But what airplane could it be? From where did it come? It was once to the left, and then to the right of the balloons, maneuvering in such graceful and effortless manner as no plane had done before. Why did it always have a circular appearance, and no outline of airplane reveal itself? Why, indeed?

It seemed to handle the situation as though it knew more than all concerned below, and apparently had its own purposes. It made no effort to come low and investigate. Rather it gradually disappeared higher and higher with the cluster. No plane could have behaved in such a manner. Higher and higher they went, until "plane" and balloons disappeared.

The state police force was appealed to, and radio and newspapers carried notices for anyone finding the balloons or cultures to report them. But nothing

He concluded definitely that Orfeo's condition came under the general classification of Constitutional Inadequacy, in an extreme degree. Also, he was the first to determine that years back the patient had been subject to trichinsis, contracted by eating contaminated pork. It had been an acute attack, and Orfeo was very fortunate to be alive. Yet this left no residue active in his more indogenic condition.

Orfeo gazed at this man in admiration. The doctor advised him never again to be occupied in anything that was not to his choice and liking; to at least minimize the burden on the nervous system. Of course, the good doctor knew this was easier said than done. Few people are fortunate enough to follow an avocation natural to their temperaments.

In Los Angeles

Orfeo found Los Angeles to be virtually free of thunderstorms. This was enough to make it home. His family saw other attractions in it .During this initial stay of five months quite a bit of Southern Calfiornia was taken in. It was the Morongo Basin in San Bernardino County, however, which was fully attractive. The desert, where geological evidences spoke, and where some sort of intermediate between the living and non-living universe met. Here he purchased a small corner lot for a future home.

The decision was made to return to Trenton, where they remained for some months, preparing at the same time to return to Los Angeles.

During this interim Orfeo published a thesis, "Nature of Infinite Entities," which included chapters as: Atomc Evolution, Suspension, and Involution—Origin of Cosmic Rays—Velocity of the Universe—A Supreme Intelligent Power. This he mailed to many universities and individual scientists working on fundamental research. This was his interest, not the capers of kings, or the "flying saucers." Facts and more facts. The virus, the atom, bacteria, static electric, the brain, metallurgy—the universe. These were things to feast upon. Flying saucers were for those who had time to waste on them. He had promised in the thesis to eventually continue it into the subjects of The Molecular Function; Thermal Dissipation; Mass Cosmos of Organisms; The Chrome Principle; Evolution and Involution of the Virus.

In the light of things to come little did he know how amateurish his efforts were. These subjects required more than writing from mere postulates and conceptions. These were not for a scatterbrain. Science was well ahead, and needed no philosophy that did not advance materially.

Orfeo longed for Frank, who could have professionally ordered and delineated his abstractions, clear into mathematics. Yet he could only remain as mute as a stone; an orphan of science.

It was time to return to their new home, Los Angeles. Here he went into business with his father. Many hardships, and a form of monopoly made the venture a vain one after three years, and much loss. Yet, the monopoly was broken and the field opened to new firms, which now increased the competition. It was finally decided to close the business.

If he would return to Trenton, comfort and a small fortune waited. But these things have small attraction for one whose world of reality is in the tiny electron, the photon, or the sunspots. Besides, there was still the lightning to reckon with. To an electro-phobic this conjecture remains paramount. Los Angeles would be home. Not too far was the desert of Morongo Basin and Twenty Nine Palms, that the entire family liked so well. The desert thundered in its quiet.

At the close of the business he was offered the opportunity by a friend to run a remodeled clubhouse, which had formerly belonged to the family of Victor McCleglan. It was ideal for Orfeo's primitive temperaments. But time and fundamentals, and his deep-rooted nervous frailty had dulled these instincts, though he took up the offer.

An Attitude Is Changed

The "flying saucers' had become things no longer ignorable, even though he remained aloof to them as yet. But the very pattern of their behaviors recalled an incident now dim in his recollection; an incident on the little farm, Albor, five years ago.

As manager of the clubhouse, he had succeeded after five months to expedite its leasing outright by a large society. He was now not employed at all. This was the end of a life that was once of some human normality. It was the beginning of one no longer grounded firmly to the earth. The past was dead.

Mabel, his wife, was now employed as manager of the snack bar of the Los Feliz Drive-In Theater, adjacent to the clubhouse. Orfeo had a year before written a script for a motion picture on space travel, our takeoff for the moon supposedly at the turn of the century, 1999. It was strictly amateur.

Suposedly the crew met another party on the moon, who

were from another world, and gone there to meet "us" as they anticipated. These other people would not reveal their origin or home, nor their actual names, but their leader said they could be called by various names, each according to an associated impression. Names as Neptune, Mars, Leo, Orion; and the women such as Vega and Lyra.

They briefly divulged bits of their secrets of health and material progress to the men from earth. Their poise and general characteristics were superb far beyond those of the earth explorers. No lasting anger did they exhibit: not even when one of the earth party accidentally caused the death of their own Orion and Lyra, when this unstable member became panicked during an emergency.

All in all it was a type of script designed to elevate the standards of space and science stories above the gadget, blood and thunder fantastics pouring so numerously into the market. But these types of stories had shown little value or financial profits, and public interest had all but faded in them. Thus, his own script lay gathering dust and forgotten. Orfeo felt that the public would never accept today any entertaining programs which are below a standard of intelligence and authenticity. The public is not so ignorant or gullible as many story-tellers want to believe.

and forehead felt as though they would burst.

Yet in this entire syndrome there was not a sign of pain. Never had his "nerves" before followed such a pattern of behavior. It seemed that death was imminent. But from what? How and when? Somehow he supported these with a measure of equanimity. Nevertheless he went outside for a time, to be near the exit gate in case he became worse.

As there was no change he continued to work, but now in some degree of apprehension. He remained rather quiet, and was asked several times what had come over him. But his only concern was to see quitting time and hurry home. Perhaps to die.

Life can be sweet at such times. Orfeo dreaded the return of years of insufferable nervous debility and symptoms, which seemed far in the past. Also, these new affairs were more persistent, more determined to break down his ingrown fortitude developed by time and trials.

The blessed whistle finally droned, and they were done for the night. His symptoms had somewhat subsided, but the deep thirst persisted, and Orfeo thought he would stop for something to drink.

He was now driving southeastward on Victory Boulevard. When he decided to stop the symptoms returned with renewed vigor, and the new onslaught

Orfeo believed for years that the entire universe teems with intelligent life, each world in its own solar system. But, as to the flying saucers (crystal discs), he still paid little attention, and brushed aside any discussion of them. Never, he thought, would these worlds actually meet one another. No, never. All that any could ever explore would be their own solar systems. And even this required forces and techniques beyond man's present conceptions, and certainly beyond his own. A narrow vision and hope this was, yet destined soon to be relegated to the past, as dead as the remainder of his past; of all the past.

Facing the prospect of employment, Orfeo made application at the Burbank plant of Lockheed Aircraft Corporation, and was taken on, starting on April 2, 1952, in metal fabrication. After six weeks some were transferred to the plastics unit, he included.

Somehow it was all as he would have it had the choice been his to make. His permanent placement was with a two-man crew working on radomes, or plastic and glass housings for the radar works of the F-94C and F-94B Starfires. Now it was a crew of three. Al, Richard and Orfeo. One a Bohemian sort of fellow, the other a typical American breadwinner, the third a scatterbrain.

was frightening. So refreshment was forgotten. He must hurry home. Also, it now seemed that his ears had become numbed, and traffic was a muffled, half-real rhythm of autos.

At Alameda Boulevard a red light stopped them. Now his forehead, temples and eyes seemed to swell up so they might burst. But still no pain was felt. It appeared that the night became brighter, as a twilight haze.

Directly ahead, and a little higher than the car, a deep red, very faint oval object came in view. It was nearly a circle. The length was about five times the daimeter of the traffic light. It held his attention, and momentarily all symptoms were forgotten.

So red it was, yet so dim, that it appeared to be removed from substance or reality.

The signal changed and traffic moved forward. The object did also, keeping its distance as an unreachable mirage. Orfeo thought it must be some peculiar function of his eyes, and looked out to the left and to the right. But the oval disc remained only in front. It were as though an unseen truck rode ahead, with only a burgundy color insigna visible. But it kept a definite true distance, noiselessly, as no truck on earth could have done.

and "souare peg in a round hole." A mixed crew, indeed.

Al and Richard were interested in news and developments. but they would believe few things which did not present themselves materially and precisely before them. Such were these two that they served well to "cushion" the newcomer in the fantastic chain of events which followed. In looking back it seems as though all the sequences of events were laid out in some sort of rehearsal by an occult destiny.

This was the swing shift, working from 4 p.m. to 12:30 a.m. A conglamoration of people, and a type of work altogether appealing.

The Road Opens

Friday, May 23, 1952. This night, at 11:00 o'clock he felt strangely ill, symptoms struck him which were not familiar ones. Between the shoulders persistent, prickly tension, as of electrical currents "leaking" out, from the spine knob located there, into the system. The right arm and hand felt it acutely. The chest seemed to well-up in a hot sensation. The heart palpitated, and was barely at the edge of pain. The back of the neck and the head became tense.

A thirst seized him, that no water could quench. His eyes

A little farther ahead Sonora and Riverside merge into Victory Boulevard, and from there it was a clear stretch of Riverside Drive. At this intersection the signal lights blink on and off in red, and a stop must be made before proceeding on.

As he stopped here all the symptoms became noticeable again. The ghostly object was on the other side of the intersection, as though waiting for him to cross over, and inteligently active. Orfeo had kept well to the right side while driving; yet some horns sounded for him to move on, and it occurred suddenly to him that no one else seemed aware of this object. Perplexed he moved on, crossing to Riverside Drive, the "burgundy companion" keeping its distance, ahead of him.

A few yards ahead a small bridge crosses the Los Angeles River, and immediately past this bridge Forest Lawn Drive goes off to the right, a rather lonely stretch of road.

The object now seemed to come closer, more visible, and for the first time "approachable." Orfeo's symptoms increased in intensity. The tenseness and heat in the right arm became "heavy." The object was now so close it seemed to be master, commanding, almost breathing. There was yet not a sound from it, but as it went to the right Orfeo was impelled to do likewise, following it on Forest Lawn Drive. He was in a way dissociated from the world, though at this point three municipalities merge: Los Angeles, Glendale, Burbank. But something, someone had complete control and guidance of him, though he was at this time benumbed as to the actual situation, and felt associated with only this object, and its ethereal origin.

About one mile down Forest Lawn Drive his "companion" impelled him to drive off the road, onto a dirt platform, on the right side. The platform ended to a seeming abrupt abyss of space, while to the left a cliff stretched upward. Between these was the road, and Orfeo was conscious of occasional traffic passing.

At once the red object eased off and away, descending some, then ascending and accelerating away. It went as a meteor, but disappeared in the sky without leaving even a spark.

Instantly something else took the place where it had just hurtled from. Two effluorescent green discs, about 30 inches apart, and each about 30 inches in diameter were there, shimmering, like two bubbles perfectly suspended in air. They appeared to be in a state of extreme agitation.

as the first time they had looked upon one of us.

These moments seemed interminable, though it is doubtful that more than three minutes elapsed during this projection. And a world of thoughts were exchanged in complete silence. He knew his were already known to them.

To think that such an experience were permitted to him. He felt ashamed, as a criminal in the presence and sight of innocent ones. Certainly he was far from deserving this.

They faded away, and there was a feeling that he and his whole environs were being swept with them, for he had lost contact even with the two circles on each side of that "screen." But there they were, with an emptiness again between them. Again the voice:

"Orfeo—you are so confused. But the ROAD WILL OPEN. Write again the "Nature of Infinite Entities." The road will open."

"I will. I know I can—very soon. Is it correct?"

"Enough. Beloved friend; the enemy is formidable, and prepares (as yet classified information). . . Again, the road will open."

"Thank you, great sir." (Orfeo waited for him to emerge in view.)

"In all the world we came to

tion.

Hardly two seconds had elapsed from the moment the burgundy color object disappeared. a most delightful masculine voice suggested. . .

"Come out here."

Orfeo stepped out from the right side door. Unafraid as yet, he closed it and stayed near to the front fender, unaware of his own movements. There were only he and these two beautiful green discs. All else was a dreamlike shadow in the background. He knew of no world of existence, past or present.

What followed is here set down in the best recollection. It can easily be gathered as. to who is, doing the talking or thinking. . .

"Orfeo, beloved friend—Greetings."

". . . Greetings"

"Do you remember us?"

"Yes, . . . I mean, Yes, indeed."

"Your balloons in New Jersey — beloved friend."   ·

(The voice was as mellow-dipped in the gold of the stars. Who could know fear at this moment?)

"Yes, I saw your plane go with them."

"They saw, but saw not. The world sees, but sees not. This you know. Orfeo, you are thirsty. Ever so thirsty. A bottle of drink for you."

On the fender of the car Orfeo "took up" a bottle, drinking the most satisfying "nectar" he had ever tasted, and thereby all symptoms and thirst vanished at once. The voice then continued.

"In all the world we came to three likely subiects to touch. One from India. One from Rome. And one from Los Angeles."

"Thank you, sir." Orfeo felt a fraternal belonging, as if the fine essences of man were one, and that he had at this moment stepped over that threshold.

"Beloved Friend—goodnight."

Nothing more. Silence and quiet. The two green circles faded perceptibly. There was a sudden darkness as the night was night again.

The Road Opens

He was alone; there was now nothing as he remained momentarily looking at the spot. This time a very faint "swoosh" rose and died at the spot where a moment ago a glowing promise was alive. It was 2:00 o'clock in the morning, and as though nothing had happened, the city lights, and all surroundings were again normal.

Two small green lights appeared in the northern sky, in the same location and proceeding in the same direction as the burgundy red disc had soared off in. They, too, suddenly accelerated and disappeared. Orfeo had the strange feeling of now not being at all associated with the phenomenon.

The realization of being here alone, for no apparent reason, and no vivid recollection of what must have been a "realistic and orderly dream." opened up seven seas of bewildering fear upon him. He rushed into the car,

"You are still perplexed. But the author of "Worlds Are Mad Tonight" should not be. Do you long to see Orion and Lyra?"

"Yes, . . . Oh, yes."

The space between the two circles gradually became visible, as of indirect lighting, and much as a television screen.

Two images emerged. from shoulders up. It is difficult to say what color hair or eyes, or any such details existed. It seemed that all hues and colors were blended in one superb end. Here indeed was a man and a woman near a possible ultimate of perfection. There were evident no trinkets, no vanities, no artifices. These exquisite personages conveyed at once a message that penetrated, even though they were silent and seemingly immobile. There was easily felt a kindness, understanding, experience, moderation. complete joy of the five senses. Life in full. All this and not a word spoken.

The only clue that they were projections of living people, and not photographs, was that their eyes were at times looking at different parts of Orfeo, not always directly at his eyes. Yet no movement had he ever detected. They appeared anxious to look him over, as in a review rather than keeping collected as best he could. while the vehicle made a sharp left U-turn. screeching and nearly overturning.

When he reached home his wife excitedly asked what was the matter with him in such a state of apprehension. Orfeo could not bring himself to tell her, and she became fearful that perhaps something terrible had happened. With great effort he laughed. and related some shadow incidents of which none were associated with the facts. She was set at ease, yet remained in a distant attitude of askance, and Orfeo wondered sincerely if he were in a twilight world between sanity and insanity.

It was a neurotic sleep for him that night, the incident vividly recalled in the usual absurdity of such dream-sleep.

Magnificent Incredibles

In the morning he awoke into a new world. In one sense reality seemed to have taken wings, while in another a new reality emerged. It were as though finding onself as the only person experiencing life, the only life in existence, and others were as phantoms and acessories in a bizzare one-man universe. Anyone finding themselves in this dissociated feeling would make every effort to get back to the material actualities; to feel secure and let others occupy the hectic fronts of events.

Two days later he returned to the scene, with his son, Richard, 12 years. Orfeo blurred off some hazy excuse for going there, which caused Richard to ask some questions.

There were many bottles lying around, but the one "out of this world' was nowhere in sight. He told Richard that he had seen here what may have been a "flying saucer," and an automobile parked. Surprisingly Richard was not too incredulous, and he pried Orfeo with questions that would do honor to an investigation official.

Raymond, 15 years old, was at home. Both, as well as their mother, had in the long past solicited Orfeo's opinion on the flying discs, receiving only indifferent and scoffing replies. Too often we ignore and ridicule our very own, and too often amends are made too late. He was beginning to pay, for a different man was beginning to emerge; with a little more consideration and feeling. It hurt to think back.

This would not be all. Events were to develop that would place him in a position nearly utterly alone. Life would flow along, and he would feel as an outside spectator, perhaps never again to feel a connected part of it.

Having returned to the scene seemed to bring a refreshing sense of reality, for he felt that the episode was something that had no substance, and would soon fall into the remote recesses of memory. He felt relief in the fact that the news and public were discussing the aerial phenomena, and somehow the picture would soon become intelligible. After all, there was science, to whom he could readily turn for practical reassurances.

May 28, 1952, work progressed as usual at the plant. At 7:30 in the evening Orfeo, another man, and a woman were working on the outside. The three of them commented on the beautiful aurora-like spectacle appearing overhead. It brought some discussion of the Aurora Borealis, or northern lights, which it resembled, and the incident was soon forgotten.

However, the whole syndrome of symptoms became faintly felt again by Orfeo. He paid little attention to them. In fact, this might prove the whole episode of five days ago merely as some function of a disturbed nervous system.

But the symptoms increased in intensity. At 9:00 o'clock they were as intense as on that other night, and he hurried outside again to be near an exit. Once more fear had gripped him.

In the skies the "aurora" was in full bloom. It began at the mountains some distance to the north, extending southwest. That was all; nothing else. The symptoms gradually subsided into warm, blessed relief, and the world, and that aurora were again good to be with.

One, or perhaps two days later a picture appeared in a daily paper of an unexplained vapor trail, and an aurora light surrounding it. It was photographed by an amateur photographer in Santa Monica.

Unexplained! Was Orfeo not to rest? Was he to be permanently tantalized? Who in his place could have ignored the sequences and events, be they fact or fancy? Who would not now recall those phantom words, "The Road Will Open?"

The next morning, on arising, things made sense again. There were automobiles, houses, people, work, play, science, religion. A little meditation on these things had an orienting effect on him.

In the afternoon he had dinner with his wife and a 5-year-old neighbor boy. He felt refreshed and relaxed. But, at 2:00 o'clock the symptoms returned, this time of a "sore throat," deep-rooted thirst, and faint background symptoms of the whole group.

He decided not to go to work.

By 3:00 o'clock all feelings and apprehensions subsided, and there was now a sense of well-being. He thought back. Just a few days ago, at this same time, he had asked his wife and younger son if they heard a droning from overhead. It was steady, unvarying for half an hour. It stopped suddenly a few minutes before he started off to work, as he felt well again.

Coincidentals! All coincidences says the realist. Perhaps so.

All Quiet For June

On June 2nd, Mabel and Richard boarded a Constellation for a trip and visit to Trenton. Orfeo hated facing three weeks without his wife and son. But laughingly he asked Richard to be on the alert, and if anything should show up he was to take a good look at details. Richard assured his dad a good report of any aerial mystery.

For all these three weeks there were hardly any mentions of flying saucers. Orfeo felt nothing of the symptoms or apprehensions. At last things had become normal.

Three weeks later, in the small hours of the morning, he and Raymond met the returning tourists at International Airport in Los Angeles. Raymond and Richard at once took up their interrupted bickerings, beginning exactly where they had left off .. .. Richard

spontaneously, from pure memory, unlimited revelations in a manner nearly professional.

He felt that he had once started something which was never completed. But, what was it? Could it be his intention to preach? Was it the story? The proposed "Mohara" desert village? Or was it something in science? All had been recently dropped by him. And which it was that now demanded attention just would not emerge into his consciousness.

The month of July turned its half-way mark, and from that point is history written with us forever. The skies seemed to open with a barrage of continuous aerial displays, and many people became convinced of interplanetary visitations, excitedly expecting a landing or some contact. Others attributed the phenomena to fulfillment soon of Spiritual Prophesies, while others to harbingers of woeful events. And there were even those who cared not one way or the other.

Orfeo welcomed the screaming headlines and reports, the public concern, and the vibrant climax of expectancy in the air, for at last the world was to share his secret and relieve him of his dilemma. Also, we would perhaps enter into a new undreamed of era of revelations. But the true fact was on the contrary, an increasing degree of his predica-

three weeks before. Richard paused long enough to say, "Hey, Dad, you make good Constellations at Lockheed. Everybody talked about them."

"We'll make them even better from now on, Son, believe me."

Richard reported. Nothing at all unusual was sighted. And had things remained in that normal state this could never have been written down.

All through June, however, Orfeo had a half serious urge to determine whether the peculiar coincidences were fact or of an illusory nature. If any material reality was in any way associated with circumstances, he would himself signal for more comprehensive contacts. Was he under "constant observation?" Such dreams he would surely not divulge to others.

All was quiet, and there was no form of response throughout the month of June. Indeed, it seemed that the signals had worked in the reverse, obliterating all incidences.

In the beginning of July the discs were emerging in the news again. He shrugged them off once again. Yet, somehow, each report reached his sub-consciousness, as though they were of his own origin. He was a duality of character, whereby he denied them on the one hand, and spoke for them on the other. They were in a sense "very close" to him. He laughed about them; yet had a respect divine for them. He

creasing degree of his predicament. America was radiant with "flying saucers," but they acted more as phantoms than as material realities.

On July 23, 1952, Orfeo failed to report for work. He just did not feel up to it. At 8:30 in the evening he walked from his house to the snack bar of the drive-in theater. He felt relieved in company. The young women attendants were speaking of flying saucers, and how their husbands would like to see even one.

Orfeo joined in the conversation, which eventually turned to a humorous and lampooning slant. There was laughter. Laughter which for him would soon come to an abrupt end. Yet, for a short while he had joined the multitudes, normal people, and saw things in their light. Then he finished a cup of coffee and started back for home, to retire for the night.

This theater has two screens, facing opposite ways, and the walk took him through the empty side facing southeast. At the other end is a lonely spot, where the Glendale boulevard and Hyperion avenue bridge spans overhead.

Half-way through the lot Orfeo felt his upper chest and throat well-up and relax rather pleasantly, and seemingly in control by someone else ,something. But there was not the slightest sense of pain nor impending doom. At once a voice, coming from his own

a respect divine for them. He could not bear to think that someone else might have been contacted; yet he laughed at the entire subject. There was a certain jealousy in him, not of the ego or selfishness, but that a precarious and sensitive situation existed, and any error or slip on the part of the flying discs, or breach by earthmen; anything would result in uncontrolled confusion. In a short time, however, it was apparent the situation was in highly expert control; errorless.

To all who would bring up the subject of the day Orfeo would listen and add his own, introducing mere glimpses of their true character, freezing them into a spector of half-belief. But only half-belief, for in a way he was in a world alone, and none was there to be met who would comprehend the actual glory, or actually believe what could really be told.

By mid-July there was a definite change in him. He felt master of any situation, and had rapidly bloomed into the person he had often hoped he could be. The secrets of the entire universe virtually opened up, with no effort on his part. Now, for the first time, he felt he could write once a voice, coming from his own vocal cords, reprimanded, citing shame on him, yet in a musical aria, said, "O-Hee-O." It was loud, smooth, gentle, and suggested a latent talent.

He smiled it off to himself; nevertheless his thoughts went immediately to the recent events, the superior beings, and eternity.

At the end of the lot he opened the corrugated metal gate and closed it again behind him. He was now alone, with the overhead concrete bridge ahead. Beyond that, so close, yet soon to be so far, the eleven unit apartments, where he resided. Here he would soon be asleep.

There seemed to be a hazy, misty obstruction between him and the arch of the bridge just ahead. It was barely visible. It was like a reproduction of a ghostly Eskimo igloo, but so transparent it hardly seemed real, so like a half-bubble of soap, with the bottom curving outward, m. like a turtle.

Almost at once a section seemed to become dark and spread out, as an inverted cone. The interior, now translucent and more real was revealed. As if in a trance, Orfeo walked to the aperture, hesitated a split second, and knew there was no alternative but to enter.

There was no sign of life, nor sound. All the recent events became realities in his consciousness again. Once more this was the only world that actually existed. Come in, be at home with people he knew but saw not.

A pearly comfort chair on the far side cozily suggested he sit here; come home. It was a pearly interior, all pearl, shimmering and tending to recede from view constantly; this dome-like, utterly empty room.

He sat down, feeling very secure and comfortable, as though he had done this before. But what would happen now? Was it perhaps to meet someone "well known" to him? How could he be so self-confident in such a situation; developing so smoothly in less time than it takes to tell it?

As he sat there the wall itself seemed noiselessly to expand and close the aperture where he had just entered, closing toward the left.

Orfeo felt completely cut off from his family and friends. Yet he felt secure, and in the hands of friends who could overcome any situation for him, and who had purposes to all that they undertook.

All sound was now shut off. The pearly interior allowed a trickle of light here and there, giving the inside a twilight, satisfying glow. He felt engulfed by a pure and esthetic environment superb.

ly, the chair or the craft, and came to rest when his position was about a quarter circle from his previous position.

Again an inverted cone aperture spread until it was approximately six feet wide at the base. This had spread from left to right. The sight revealed was one of awe. A tremendous, brilliant rainbow haloed around a huge mass of darkness.

Again the crystal craft or the seat turned to the left, and a new aperture appeared, slightly to the right of the first, adding about three more feet to the base of the previous opening.

His head and eyes became tense. There was a return of the now familiar symptoms, and the dark mass became lighter, a beautiful twilight of blue intensity. The full circle of rainbow was now in view, except a bit at the bottom, which was obstructed by the floor line. A sight defying description this was: the whole earth stood before him. The whole mass seemed to shimmer, in spite of the dark hue. And the Western Hemisphere of the globe was discernable. Indeed, the radiant rainbow was the scope of our atmosphere.

For a moment Orfeo suspected that he was dying: that all this was the final upheaval and billowing away of life. Yet it was constant and sustained a phenomenon that would not be to an ebbing life.

THE TRANSFORMATION

A low vibrant hum, more felt than heard, took on a crescendo and he felt gently "pushed" against the comfortable chair; pushed by every inch of his body, as though his body were pushing backward beyond any control on his part.

The interior became dark, as though some great shadow engulfed the entire dome. The floor seemed as solid as if it were the ground itself, vibrating deep, hidden currents of the earth, in a gentle, constant flow. The sensation of push against the chair by his body did not increase. But neither did it cease.

Reason began to take form, and a grip of fear was beginning to overpower him, when an orchestration, of one of his favorite songs gradually arose. It was "Fools Rush In" where angels fear to tread; an exact transcription of the Voices of Walter Schuman. The strains had an orienting effect on Orfeo, for it lent a thread of association. Memories returned to him in a conglamorate sensibility.

Soon the interior lighted up softly again. Orfeo noticed how his soiled work clothes, which he was wearing, stood in bold and ugly relief in this exquisiteness He felt that his entire body and soul were equally unfit to be privileged such divine, visual. realistic a dream.

He felt so well and comfortable that he gave but scant thought to the possibility of the air diminishing, or becoming toxic. He gave little thought to anything, but the developing of things at hand. The soothing

Furthermore, there were none but normal physical sensations, except the faint but familiar symptoms, and memories of associated events of recent days vividly conscious.

In all this a voice arose—the voice superb.

"Beloved Friend, see your home, Earth. Is it not a bosom of peace and beauty? You would not be concerned from here. What occurs there is the concern of them only—and you."

For many years Orfeo had been unable to come to tears. But at this point they came from an overwhelming swell of emotion that seemed to purify and cleanse; transforming him from a hardened reasoner into a more feeling individual.

"Weep, Orfeo, for we join you at this moment."

There was a slow turning to the right, until the earth was removed from the scene. At the aperture there was now a teeming mass of stars—seemingly so close that they might be but a few feet distant. Large and small, single and clustered, red and amber, and many hues. It seemed that at any moment one would suffocate in this closeness; this fairyland luminescence.

Eyes still wet, Orfeo thought. Expert hands were behind all this, and would see him safe even beyond and above their own safety. Meteors were nowhere seen or evident. In all this setting his immutable awareness of the Supreme God dawned to comfort him. Could God at this moment be conscious of these incomprehensible events? Would

things at hand. The soothing music played on ethereally as his body seemed to push back on the chair perpetually. His thoughts were not of the past, nor of his wife, sons, or other relatives, but of the immediate present — and minutes ahead.

The musical rendition neared its end. What then? Was he to spend an eternity in this pearly igloo? The body now seemed to gradually relax its backward push against the seat, until it ceased.

At the same time the music came to an end. The smooth vibration of the floor also slackened some, but this did not stop completely. It was surely evident that some motive power was housed somewhere in the floor. Orfeo thought of the incident on Forest Lawn Drive, and that perhaps he was carried there again, to continue the "dream" to a more tangible comprehension. There was complete quiet, and fear was impossible under the circumstances.

———

Then something turned smooth-comprehensible events? Would God for even a fleeting moment center attention on so insignificant a living being? After all, Orfeo had learned that even every hair of everyone were counted and pre-ordained, and each atom and molecule was registered and pre-destined. God seemed so close and so active here, yet concerned with all else but him. He felt secure.

———

Just then, a huge ship, like a dirigible came emerging from the right. It ignored the stars and bodies "in its path" and proceeded forward. It seemed that the stars and bodies gave way without moving to its progress. It was indeed as a large dirigible, but flattened at the bottom.

It is difficult to conclude as to the actual material of its structure. It appeared to be metallic, yet could very likely be of a crystal-metal-plastic composition. Its light control properties definitely suggested perfect crystal alloyed throughout. To all appearances the size of the craft was not less than 900 feet long, and at lease 90 feet high.

As he pondered this "close-in" universe, and the elegant ship, the voice spoke again. It was now accompanied by music that could have originated from all space, from every remote recess of space. In full view was this half-ethereal ship, and it suggested that all sound and action eminated from its interior.

"Brother of a man. Ask no longer why we have chosen you. Each is divinely created. But a child shall lead, and the meek are strong; dirt is clean, and sickness as but a gem. Atheism is a frigid end; hypocracy an unseen venom. All is one; bad, good; evil, holy; past, future. You are on one side or the other, always. We know where you stand. Why, Beloved Friend, are you apathetc and inactive? You, a chosen one. Who is so mildly cosmic; you, so expendable. Is your life to flash away as nothing?"

"No! Please, no. I am not such a one who cares not. My very life is yours. I beg to see you, Neptune, or Orion. Give me health, and there is nothing I cannot accomplish for you. Do this. Let me forever feel as I feel now. Ask the Almighty this in my behalf."

But the ship began to move leftward, and upward. One porthole after another opened in rapid flash successions as it ascended, until three complete flights, as decks. became radiant from indirect lighting with only pearly bits of an interior showing. Nothing more.

At the bottom, two large rotars, one near each end of the great craft, revealed themselves: deep, radiant green color imminating from both rotars. How well Orfeo remembered their identical forms on lonely Forest Lawn Drive. His own craft began a leftward turning. Again the tremendous rainbow came in view, and the earth within it. Puffs of faint light dotted the earth, cities in the night.

Suddenly three "flying saucers" darted from nowhere, and sped forward, coming to rest in fixed positions. At once it was' apparent that these positions were what would be Capernaum, Moscow and Washington. And from the one at Washington flew out two more; one coming to rest over Rio de Janiero, the other over Los Angeles. The one at Los

Angeles gave birth to another, which settled over Tokyo. Six beautiful discs, with green main centers, and amber light halo fringes. The scene was one that mythology would blush to dare contrive up. There came no sound from anywhere. All was quiet as could be.

In this solitude and glory Orfeo formed his own conclusions, his own befogged interpretations, with a power not of his control. All the crystal discs and their placements seemed to indell a message easily decipherable, telling more history than al our compiled data.

Los Angeles. Oddly he felt that he had been there before, not too long ago. That he had left that city a little more than half an hour before was not in his recollection. And at once, by some remote control, all the crystal discs sped away into invisibility: except two: one at the point of Capernaum, the other at Los Angeles. And the grand voice returned:

"The road you have explored for your own satisfaction has opened. Widen it as it will be widened for you. Strain to think. Nature of Infinite Entities must be fully developed. The enemy does not wait. Dream on. But act—act, Orfeo."

"I will."

"A privilege divine has been yours. A power shall be yours."

"Thank you."

"We love your home. Find it interesting, and also love it for what you now know."

The crystal disc at Los Angeles went the course of the others. There was only the one at Capernaum, and the smaller aperture on the right of the craft began to close noiselessly, as the velvet voice resumed.

"Home, beloved, tortured one.

Page 4. Column 5.

Home, Orfeo. And yet one question remains in you; dreamer-doubter. We know. You ask if the Star of Bethlehem was. Now you know. It was—it never extinguished."

The large aperture closed rapidly. Again his body seemed to push delightfully against the back of the seat. And the strains of the Lord's Prayer, as we know it, filled the dome. In this magnificent setting Orfeo felt as a worm of a human being; dirty, unkempt, and sinful in the fullest sense.

Ah, indeed! He was chosen because he was the most expendable; the most useless in the eyes of destiny, not the most loved. Yet these beings spoke as though they loved him deeply. How much must they love the others?

The strains of the Lord's Prayer seemed to wash away these unhappy reflections of the conscience as rapidly as they arose. Through the strains the voice spoke:

"Beloved friend, we baptize you by all the spectral forces we know."

A white beam flashed through the pearly wall of the dome craft and seared Orfeo just above the stomach and below the left breast. There was a flashing pain: then partial oblivion, in which he could only remember the musical ensemble.

metal was found there that is out of this world. It is now on the quiet, very secret... Orfeo, how many will show up tonight?... When will they land?... Ask one to land near my house and I will believe all there is to them.

Orfeo now remained silent to all these. He could not remember having engendered or provoked this lampooning, except in the usual small talk. In a way it was relieving, for he felt many were sharing his dilemma, and soon the big news would happen. Yet the innermost secrets were irrevocably his own, and none would believe even the merest detail of anything he started to say. In the news of the weeks the hoaxers, dreamers, and egotists had their followers. Yet he could pick up not the slightest serious believer. But never would he, nor could he treat the subject openly in the average level of conversation.

He resumed his solicitous signals into the sky. Never was there any response. And his feeling that all his recent "experiences" might, after all, have been illusion, or some bizzarre nervous behavior, or a self-evolved realistic figment of the imagination took hold again. Yet, he could not attribute his new ability of clear and boundless thought, his greater ability to write completely without notes or outlines to imagination, or nervous upheavals. And there

The prayer ended, but a new strain of countless violins seemed to envelope all space, while all the past events flashed vividly in his remaining consciousness, in every fiber of the body. This was like Eternity itself. It would be a blessing if he could remain in such a catalepsy forever, he felt

Gradually the music subsided and equally he seemed to wake from the half-sleep. The push of his body against the back of the seat also eased. Again there was a turning, apparently back to the original position. Then quiet and still, but for the soft vibration of the floor. The wall again opened in the same inverted cone shape. There were the environs of the theater grounds, as though he had never moved from the position when the craft had left.

"Goodnight."

These were the last words from the voice. Orfeo knew he must leave: reluctantly, slowly, from this "home." He walked out and circled to the right of it, and for an instant his glance had left the craft. As he looked for it again it was now in the air, as a faint half-bubble, hardly visible. Suddenly it was not there at all. He looked for even a sign of it; and then a "flying saucer" appeared in the northeast sky, a red disc turning instantly to deep green, and soared off into seeming eternity.

was one peculiarity. As the essences were written down they were again lost to him, and only the abilities remained which made possible things yet to be written. As though he were consuming something, and only the unused remained vividly before him. Normally it would have been impossible for him to elaborate the "Nature of Infinite Entities." Real or fancy, he was a transformed man.

———

Orfeo had often been to the Griffith Observatory, not far off, and to Mt. Wilson above Pasadena. He liked the atmosphere of astronomy which these points suggested and eminated.

It was Saturday evening, and he had driven to the Griffith Observatory, perhaps for some orienting influence. The sun had almost set completely as he looked at the panorama of sprawling Los Angeles, with the darkening Pacific to the right distance, and Mt. Wilson in the shadows of the left. It was a grand panorama. But therein was embodied the world that preyed upon itself for existence, in hardly civilized fashion. The world was here represented, indeed.

Ideal shared place with larceny in man. From the highest medical circles and theological estates, to the one on skid row.

He felt an urge to go to the snack bar just ahead, and talk with someone. But talk of what? How could he make sense? Home was the best place: to sleep, a fitful, restless sleep this night. It did not dawn then that that he was never again to know peace and rest from the no man's land between two worlds.

Tormented throughout the night he rolled and tossed in actual pain, and the brain burning with feverish visions. By late next morning these had subsided into but shadow residues of sensations, now centered on the left side of the chest in a localized burn-itch. As he scratched this the baptismal words rang clearly in mind. But this was a new day, alive with a reality now alien to him. Yet the personal experience of only last night were even more alien in a way.

He reflected as he rubbed the sore spot, "Bunk! All Bunk! But he was already a changed human being, literally transformed, the "flying discs" becoming the only real things that he knew of.

In the aircraft plant most of the talk was now of the "flying saucers."

. . . Well, did you read of the saucers seen at such a place? . . . Hey, Orfeo, did you know about this one? . . . Listen, did you read of the little green men in Texas or New Mexico? And some

There was as much reprehensible evil as there was good. One must give way. Groups, cliches, and citadels with tentacles returning back upon their own orgiins; man for man, man against man. All willing to allow one to ravage another, let things go by, and hope for a better tomorrow. Willing to be apathetic, while a fundamental enemy is swelling into a terrible, dark menace, to some day awake us to realities.

Yes, indeed. Fundamental evil is always equal to fundamental good. When one relaxes the other will loom up. Action and reaction is the rule of the "autoclave" of the universe. A train of such reflections seemed to run continuously within him, as the evening darkened into night.

Above was endless space, where visitors seemed in his recollection to have made themselves manifest. Indeed, words came vividly in his memory. Words from a most endearing voice:

"The enemy prepares."

The details rang clearly in his mind. How gently commanding it had spoken.

There was only one fundamental enemy Orfeo was aware of. Communism. This was the tide that was swelling into a black wall on all horizons, and must sooner or later be dealt with. The free world could hardly resist at this time **an onslaught launched** by surprise and strength by — the enemy.

The echo of the warning became more significant and meaningful. He was in complete awareness and agreement with them. But what could he do? He was but a frail and helpless human being.

Ponderingly he started back home; something might arise in his mind. Yet the only course of action seemed to be to discuss the "preposterous matter" with the proper authorities, even if they would merely think that something had snapped in his cranium.

Over the telephone he spoke with various organs of our defense. Two offices took no stock at all. It was a great relief to him that the others, the important ones seemed to be very much interested. But he continued to drive home the message to various official and non-official organizations to be sure it would not die out. (The details, obviously cannot be divulged herein.) Subsequent news items revealed that the information had a resounding impact, or that our own systems had come upon some secrets of the enemy. It matters little which had occurred. Orfeo had suddenly put into action mere words, which had been transmitted through an "ethereal mist," beyond which seemed to exist another world.

———

Behind the scenes of the flying discs a mission was given to one who might have been the least likely selected by ourselves. After having phoned the various offices of our defense forces, Orfeo went to the theater's snack

affairs, silly space drama, to religious unrealities. Time would tell. But he no longer cared for time, for the interval was heavy upon him. He forgot that he was an expendable, sacrificed long weeks before, living neither in one world nor the other. He wanted to blazon out the reality of space visitations. But he was powerless; unbelieved by all on earth, and assisted by none of the visitors.

———

This was the state of affairs on Saturday night, August 2nd, when he was again helping in the snack bar. At 11:00 p.m. he walked outside and spotted a blinking light over a hill to the west. He called those who would come out to see it, as it remained motionless in the sky above a hill. It was not so spectacular, and the others losing interest soon returned to their respective places. Orfeo remained fixed upon it, while some said it was merely a street lamp or some helicopter hovering motionless in the air.

Then the light began to move away. He called them back, saying, "there goes your street lamp." To give the benefit of the doubt to the doubters in this instance, let us write it off as a helicopter. Again Orfeo felt so disoriented that he decided to leave and go directly home, for no apparent reason.

The dark archway of the bridge seemed large, yet welcoming to him because of the memories of it. There was a certain eternal communion here, and he enthralled to it as he came under.

Just beyond was home, comfort and rest.

bar to help the others.

At exactly 10:45 a meteor-like object came into sudden being, racing southeasterly in a perfectly horizontal path. It remained perfectly round, no tail, amber light and no other color. Then it accelerated into a still more terrific speed, and disintegrated in a forward flurry of sparks, as given off by a grindstone in high action.

Two night later, Monday, July 28th, at 8:23 a similar one occurred over the aircraft plant in Burbank. This, however, was radiantly green in color, with the amber halo fringe. There was a dark overcast in the sky, ending directly overhead in a circular arch. The edge of this was grazed by sunlight, causing a beautiful horizontal rainbow to skirt these clouds.

Where the right end of the rainbow ended overhead the green-amber disc, larger than the full moon, seemed to hurtle from nowhere, grazing the ceiling of the cloud overcast, and going through some that hung slightly lower than the main ceiling. It disintegrated in the same flurry of sparks spread out forward as the previous one. Quite a few employees had observed this spectacular one. Even its slowest velocity was in the thousands of miles per hour. Orfeo was a normal spectator to this one. There were no symptoms, contacts or manifestations of any kind.

Orfeo saw in the dark overcast, arched overhead with a rainbow fringing it almost a replica of his spectacle of the earth from the interior of the crystal craft. The "flying saucer" was identical to those darting in space before him on that trip.

A man was coming from the opposite way in the darkness toward him. Orfeo felt an urge to stop him, talk with him, to unburden himself, no matter what the stranger might think. It suddenly struck Orfeo that this man came from a corner which had no entrance, but that he had perhaps been waiting. Before he could become alarmed, the stranger spoke, without halting his progress:

"Greetings, Orfeo!" It was the beautiful voice.

"And greetings to you, good sir . . . I mean, uh . ."

"You probably recall one, Neptune? Or do you not? Come and you will see—and hear."

"Neptune! You have come to give me health and strength?"

"Come, beloved one. You and I must give, not receive."

Orfeo automatically turned and followed Neptune, who had not hesitated nor once looked directly at him. Yet there was complete joy and serenity radiated from Neptune, as one who had found a long lost brother. As though he were a power station the same feeling was transmitted to Orfeo. Both their steps were clearly heard by Orfeo as they walked through the gravelled yard, and came upon a sharp bend of Glendale boulevard.

In this more lighted area Neptune's apparel at once struck Orfeo. It was one uniform shade, fitting in perfect tailoring. There seemed to be hardly a joint or seam. Never; not once did the whole suit or person fully emerge, but rather it seemed to waver, spots appearing and disappearing, as the surface of a lake in the moonlight, gently rolling. Only the face and hands were immo-

him on that trip.

THE MISSION

Thousands of people looked upon the great numbers of aerial phenomena as observations of intelligent beings from somewhere out in space. But the one person in all the world who was absolutely certain must temporarily be quiet, for he could otherwise accomplish only one end, and that would be alienation of everyone from him, including his close friends and family. But he now longed to tell it all, so the cup would pass into more capable hands.

If he did so the believers would be the first to scorn the facts. For oddly, there were fanatical believers of various shades. But most of these had limited imaginations, from mere gadgeteering the face and hands were immobile. Traffic went past and turned on the sharp bend here, and headlights were fully cast upon both as they proceeded forward. Orfeo wondered what Neptune looked like to these folks going by.

At this point the nature of this presence suddenly dawned on him; and again he felt removed from earthly reality. It was only Nptune's words and personality that kept Orgeo from breaking, as they proceeded down the sharp concrete slope of the Los Angeles River. Near the bottom Neptune suggested they sit, with a mere gesture. Then he spoke:

"Many see us as you do, and we have not even disturbed them. Your enemy prepares yet. Millions in your land will fight to the end, for your land and ideals. Millions of the globe will fight to the end for eternal ideals. Are these worth to sacrifice for?"

"Yes, indeed. And I will give my life itself, always."

"Not enough. Your life must forever give its fullness."

And for the first time he turned full gaze on Orfeo. It was a resplendid face. Eyes that knew joy, sorrow, and understanding beyond any of his own. Orfeo felt stupid, unkempt, and utterly helpless. He felt again as a hypocrite these moments.

"We also have differences, but not fundamentally. I have broken a divine code, and it shall be amended by me so it will not have been broken at all. The code of hands off; on interference in the ways of Earth. And you shall see amends made, and my repentance. I would shake your hand, but in token it must not be. Also, by having already gone too far, we pay by receding an equal degree. Thus, none will believe you, nothing will occur in greater speed than had nothing happened between us. The signs and the ways of God are for those who discern. But they are immutable, and will not change their substance or time."

"Beloved Neptune. My life, my blood, my comfort, my everything shall be regarded by me as to be given in a way to cause no added shame to me, and glory to you; if it could be so." Orfeo hardly knew he was speaking in Neptune's own contagious manner.

"We have made but one contact, Orfeo. It must not fail for any weak link. None other can be made at the time. All you know is so, and all doubts leave in that trickle of water there. The road is opened; walk it as you will. Your demise is also mine. But I smile on you with love for your enhanced numbers. Millions that will rise, and meet the great battles, with but a shred on their side for victory."

(This was a speaking of a double essence.) No one would believe on the one hand, and Orfeo was to reveal the true nature of the visitors on the other hand. Only minds atuned to the innermost secrets of nature could gather their full portents.)

Neptune gracefully extended his hand to hold Orfeo's. Orfeo recoiled his own away. And Neptune smiled on him as he spoke:

"You and I, as one; see? We would not break the code. How you have transformed. Our trust rests in you. Did we not baptize you by neutral functions? You are an apostle in that degree that you will be. And you will cleanse me from any contact with this ground, or I die unhappy."

"Think back, beloved friend. In May you cecased many persuits, and became fixed as another person. Think back, and therein is your light."

As a flash, Orfeo saw what he meant. His pet "Mohara Desert Club" had been abruptly dropped by him in May. Interest in science, and any plans for the future had ceased to exist. Yet he was soon to be completing the Nature of Infinite Entities. His energy ray description sent to the government had been forgotten. Yet this could be perfected into unlimited ranges. All but the "flying saucers" had been forgotten by him. Now he could see the meaning of Neptune's words, that he, Orfeo, knew certain things, and that these were so.

The ether exists, then. We can go forward to undreamed of ends. Indeed, to be in the future as Neptune, Orion, Lyra. At this point Neptune continued as if reading every detail of Orfeo's thoughts.

"Of God, and the ether, we too can only hypothize; like children. Children are new people. Think always on them. There is the light. For we shall soon go back to insignificance from your earth, yet never far away; to return. but not to you, beloved friend."

There was a slight pause. Then he spoke again:

"I am thirsty, Orfeo, and it is your turn." He smiled warmly.

"Oh, yes, great sir! I will get you some—uh, some refreshment. Wait here."

Neptune smiled as Orfeo went

off. On the other side of the archway he glanced back to see if Neptune was confortable, for he had left him unceremoniously. He had arisen and was looking toward Orfeo, who then climbed up the steep concrete bank. From the top he glanced again, and in the center arch there seemed to be an "igloo" of haze. Only eyes that had once seen and become familiar with such could have made out the crystal craft, as though suspended under the ceiling of that arch. Now he was in a hurry, and it was difficult to control his impatience in the nearby store. With two bottle of lemon soda he hurried back.

The craft was gone from under the arch, and soon it was clear that Neptune also had disappeared. It was not too surprising, for Orfeo had such a premonition when he had left for the refreshments. The place was now desolate, and the loneliness heavy. He glanced in the sky expectantly, and was rewarded by the appearance of a faint, small green light, which proceeded away and southeastward, along Riverside Drive.

Orfeo sat down, feeling somewhat deserted, and with a train of endless questions. What was his true name? Where were they from? Why not leave something tangible with him? How could he now go on alone? Why did he have no one to turn to who would blieve him? How could their discs, ships, and any of their manifestations be so adroit and swift in our atmosphere?

were young ladies whose husbands would give much to see even one ' flying saucer," but who themselves were luke warm on the subject. Especially Anne, a practical, energetic little worker.

"Hello, Anne. Business is quiet isn't it."

"Where were you until now?" asked Mabel, his wife.

'Oh, as usual; around the neighborhood,' Orfeo answered. Funny, he thought; but Anne had not answered him, not even noticed him. She had gone back to a section of the counter and rested her chin in her hands, looking toward the bridge.

"Were you home just lately, Orfeo?" Anne had noticed him after all.

"Yes; I just now came down."

' Well, did you see somebody welding some electric wires over there?" she asked.

"No, I didn't." Orfeo was now riveted to the conversation.

"Well, they were. At least it looked tike that. A green flare staying right there, like a cone, or torch. I was sure someone was repairing electric wires. But it was a flare — and stayed in one place; like a torch, but green all over. Then it shot away and went out."

'Anne, tell me; could an ordinary flare, or welding light behave like that?"

Ann looked at Orfeo and reflected. Then spoke with some apprehension.

"That's right, isn't it? What do you suppose it was?"

"Well, Anne! At last you've seen a flying saucer."

Came the new day just the same. Newspapers and radio, magazines and television; and conversation, all on the 'flying saucers" and their incredible behavior. Clearly the words rang in memory, "the road will open." Indeed it had. But it would not open as wide as Orfeo hoped. The speculation of everyone seemed so amateurish to him, yet he could not pry open their eyes.

But he was becoming more and more oriented. It suddenly dawned on him that Neptune had always spoken in perfect American English. This was in accord with his own fiction script, "Worlds Are Mad Tonight." He had certainly been endowed with a perception never known to him before. Had he not been given signs and material manifestations? Never mind what people would think or believe. Go on — write, write, for he at least now felt the ability and power to do so. Preach, and go on, regardless. He was an expendable, whose best had been now relegated to the past. Even the flower of the land was this moment being expanded, giving its all in Korea. It must not be in vain. Even the Son of Man was expended. That was enough.

It seemed that an end had come to it all, for the next few days were fruitless of any events. Yet the reports of 'flying saucers" continued thick and fast, and much lampooning accompanied them.

seen a flying saucer.

"No, it was more of a flare. Somebody must have been welding."

That is all she would say. Yet there was a lingering doubt in her mind, as she recalled its behavior. Orfeo walked outside.

'Farewell, beloved friend." The exquisite voice again; low and controlled. It sounded just overhead, in spite of the many cars and people around.

Bob, an attendant, and Richard, Orfeo's son, were close by and looked toward him, asking what he had said. Orfeo pretended he was merely feeling fine in this atmosphere, and had started to sing. Then looking up he saw a 'meteor" again, in the horizontal dash, and disintegrating as two had done before.

He walked home, resolute that writing would begin, no matter what the effort.

This night he spent in reflecting on questions. Why was he never to be contacted again? Why had it been him these months? Why not someone more likely and able? If he were the one selected, why then was he expendable? When will they campaign again, and who would be the contact then? If men were prepared would the meeting of two worlds then occur on a large scale? Questions by torrents, yet to each he seemed to have a shade of an answer; schedule and purpose behind them all.

The following day he obtained

August 18th he felt not well, and did not go in to work. The sun was setting when he decided to go to the scene at the bank of the river, and recall the incident again. It was lonely, but to him it remained vibrant with a livingness merging from all the universe. Had not Neptune sat here?

"Neptune," he thought. "Neptune. You had sat here with me not long ago. If I could but see a small sign. Any sign to direct me. And all his uneasiness and bodily sensations seemed to center on the healing scab on the left side of the chest as he rubbed to ease it. The fact flashed to him suddenly — the baptism.

Orfeo stood up and hurried home to investigate this seriously for the first time. It was there sure enough. It impressed him as a hydrogen atom superimposed by another, and above them a torch-like affair. He now felt vibrant with a clear job ahead. White — write — write only those things you know, in the only manner you know.

Relieved and oriented he sauntered down to the snack bar. Here paper and began to write. It was a peculiar ability, the same as in Nature of Infinite Entities, whereby the used seemed forgotten, and only the new remained vividly. All he wrote, except some details so fantastic and incredible that he decided to keep them to himself, and do not appear herein.

They say the truth will out. This surely will. For there will be no mass contacts except on these levels and this agency. There will be no large scale fundamental progress in any branch of science except through the keys and clues of Nature Of Infinite Entities, in spite of its utter simplicity. Reveal these presents to the children, New People, and the universe will unfold to us.

The space visitors have been here for some ages, and will be here in increasing measure. As a gesture to divine order of things they have forsaken their first contact forever. The glory to come belongs to all others.

It is the faith, the light, and thereby the love that we must discern in order to see clearly through those who would ravage them. We have differences among us. But these will be resolved to concordance. As brothers we awake into a new day, forgetting the hurts. For if your home is afire, many will risk life to help you. If you are drowning, many will jump in to save you. If you are hungry, many will feed you. If you bleed there is blood from thousands on hand. Fundamentally, we are brothers and sisters.

There is a distracting force, which will be met at Armageddon. In this struggle we must stand as one; no matter what comes, or how. The clouds are in the horizons, dark, ominous. But at the edges are the rainbows. both, infinite and eternal.

As for Orfeo, the implications are clear. Only with a measure of divine respect can he recall the events. His own reference to the names, given by himself, to the beings mentioned will be only under the most dignified circumstances, or not at all.

He discerns communism as a fundamental enemy, a necessary evil, given to us as are venemous creatures, the blights, the famines, the tyrannies, all incorporate in a segment of humanity; to be like the others, one day deciphered, combatted and vanquished.

Orfeo now knows why they made the choice of contact which they did. It will never be dishonored or slighted.

Arise, you Children; for of you is the New Era. Let your voices ring out in song, "WELCOME SPACE VISITORS."

into space or the atmosphere. The platinum does this superbly.

He never noticed it, but Orfeo felt that somewhere must be the "heart," or the "distributor," a perpetually active part, using a radioactive material as the initial activator. Regardless of their diameter or size, the crystal discs may vary in thickness from inches to a few feet.

At will of those in control, they can be disintegrated in two ways: by explosion or by implosion. Both would be of a high speed rate, yet slower than the explosion of either powder or the atom bomb. This is why they may burst in a white flash, or simply disappear before one's very eyes; and never emit a sound. The energy is rapidly dissipated away in the ultra-violet or the infra-red radiations, in a manner simply penetrating the surrounding atmosphere.

So ingeniously is the light diffusing property of the ships or the discs achieved, that one may hover over one's head and never be seen casually, in day or night, unless the senses were stimulated or sensitized.

The "flying saucer" or crystal disc, not only can relay whatever is emitted to it from the mother ship, but it is able to receive impressions precisely as they appear in its scope, and relay them to the mother ship, to be permanently recorded on other crystal "brains."

Their activated molecules receive and convert energy inherent in all the universe, in the form of light rays, photons, magnetic and gravitational waves. In

SPACE VISITORS."

Their Power and Structure

The crafts and missiles of our space visitors have one outstanding characteristic. They are impelled and controlled by "tapping into" universal forces. Even to us these forces are beginning to reveal themselves in our slow trial-and-error, and theoretical progress.

To understand their mechanism let us return to one of their functions.

From the very first experience with them, Orfeo was seized by strange neurological symptoms, right inside the aircraft plant. Driving home his head and eyes felt those peculiar wellings up, and the night became somewhat lighter. It was only then that the red object became visible to him. The answer did not loom to him until the symptoms were repeated various times, and nothing else occurred to distract his attention from them.

Somebody or something was able to focus radioform waves adapted to our nervous systems.

They were able to expand the pupils of the eyes and sensitize the retina so that the disc became visible to him. Simultaneously they are able to increase the activity of the brain cells, and control the entire nervous system of one within given limits. These are but a small fraction of the functions of the objects we have come to term as "flying saucers." They are guided by the mother ship, and their entire netic and gravitational waves. In short, the whole universe is a closed feed back circuit, potential at every minute point, in space or in matter. The great medium, the only true form of matter is the Ether. All else are vacuums therein, or waves caused by the vacuums.

The force of magnetic and gravitational waves is infinitely greater than we have ever surmised. Thus the maneuverings and accelerations of the flying discs is no longer a mystery. In space they can gradually attain a velocity near the region of the speed of light.

If directed accordingly, these discs can pick up the radiations of one's very thought so accurately that the train of thought is relayed to a more permanent crystaloid with extreme finality.

Their ships follow four outlines, as do the flying discs. These are the oblong, the hemispheres, the spheres, and the disc form. Any other shape may be configurations of numbers of these.

THE END

Catch Them If You Can

Any high efficiency cameras poised to snap their secrets, any orders given even in silence; any guns trained and ready for them on our speediest aircraft shall never phase them. But soon we shall begin to photograph them, see them, hear them, and bit by bit come materially upon them. Only when the time is right, and only when they gradu-

scope of power and motion can be gathered from Nature Of Infinite Entities, which is too involved to explain here.

Most of the Crystal Discs have a circular shape. They can be of various sizes, depending on their purpose. Their outer rim is motionless, or it can rotate in the opposite direction from the center. There is barely a hair gap between the two sections.

In these simple structures are all the complexities one could think of. Indeed, these are the perfect "synthetic brains."

They are made up of a perfect crystal as the main functioning substance, suspended in a super-tough plastic, which also suspends copper and platinum in molecular form; the two diffused in spiral tentacles, diminishing outward. These spirals accentuate the magnetic fluxes, disburse them to the crystal substance. Heat and friction which is accumulated is converted into partial electrical energy and conveyed to the edges. The metal spirals, pinpoints at this region emit the energy back ally "surrender" their substance to us.

They know every secret placement of a camera, every cautious telescope, every intention to perceive them with tangible proof.

Even Captain Mantell with his pursuit squadron over the government airfield were as mere amateurs. Yet Captain Mantell is probably the first, and the only one to have lost his life to the direct action of "flying saucers." Not because he might have come upon their secret, but as a token, the sacrfiicial lamb of the order. For all tangible changes shed blood, and his may have been the drop in the greatest change of all time. He too, was expendable.

The 200-inch Hale Telescope at Mt. Polomar was not to be trifled with by training it upon the moon. But in the month of October, 1952, days were spent in its rovings upon the moon, jupiter, saturn, mars, and into our solar system. For what reason was its time so wasted- Why did they leave the probings of the outer universe for such a long time, when it can spend ages in the outer reaches?

Was it to perhaps come upon some outpost of our space visitors? What were the results? They came up with nothing at all. Yet when we least expect it, and from someone we may not look to, will come intermittent bits of revelations. To them, every man, woman and child is a supreme entity.

Postscript

There are straws in the wind that point to scientific steps which are in the direction of real fundamental progress, and they should be followed up relentlessly.

One of the most important of these seems to have been buried in news as just peculiar behavior of matter, and some of it is quoted as follows:

"Exploration of the bizarre world of extreme cold has started to pay dividends. This the region between about minus 300 degrees Fahrenheit to absolute zero, the ultimate cold possible, at minus 459 degrees.

"Through this temperature change properties of matter seem radically changed, but hitherto this has been of chief interest to laboratory physicists."

The item was disclosed by the Arthur D. Little Company, of Cambridge, Massachusetts, and they look forward to added information along this line. The article goes on to say:

"A potentially useful product is a refrigerated crystal to pick up radio signals too faint to be detected by a heated tube."

"Through some metals at very low temperatures, known as super-conductors, an electric current will flow indefinitely, once it has been started."

There is an item that once might have been merely a scientific curiosity. But, that last paragraph contains one of the most important fundamental revelations of today. It completely substantiates the "universal forces" of magnetic lines, and free energy, pervading the entire expanses of the substance, Ether. This is delineated in Nature Of Infinite Entities.

Distance and Acceleration

To this moment it is difficult to determine the distance between the craft in which he sat and the earth. Orfeo is not certain.

Some of the far-flung places could hardly have been included because of the curvature of the earth. They were not merely alluded to by the "flying discs," which shot forward and came to a halt over them, but the "cities" mentioned were clearly visible. However, he was not aware of these places until the discs hurtled forward and over them. Perhaps the discs were able even to defract or resolve light in a way to focus them to his eyes. Only perhaps.

Another factor not easily explained is the distance he hovered from the earth. It must surely have been 1000 miles to see the entire sphere, and this distance reached in not more than five minutes.

There could be one explanation for the human body to receive such an acceleration. If magnetic and gravational waves are made to converge in a given area, and moved forward with an object, every molecule and atom of the matter in the area would be impelled forward in that rate of velocity. Thus any acceleration would be greatly neutralized, or even non-existent.

Another explanation may be that all impressions were perhaps mentally induced by the beings upon Orfeo, and that he probably never left the earth in the first place. With this theory he has no faith or explanation, and abhors it in the face of the facts involved.

We can take this aspect of his experiences at face value. Or we can discount them all. He can only present all as he experienced them. To Orfeo, all matter, motion and time has a physical property at its root. Clarify these, or we know nothing.

The Real Things Are Yet to Come

Their next large campaign will be more revealing than the one of 1952. We shall not only begin to hear them, and see them more definitely, but they will make themselves manifest in many forms and shapes, and cause unexplained incidences. Welcome these.

Officials and reporters will make every effort to screen out hoaxes and hysteria. They have done this very well in the past, and it is reported that only 2% of reports could possibly have been hoaxes. This is an incredibly wonderful efficiency.

Most of the scientists and officials are of the conviction that only superior intelligent beings could have been behind the behaviors of the aerial phenomena. Very few, and certainly stodgy ones, have the opinion that all could be explained as atmospheric phenomena and mass hysteria, whatever these may be. There is no question that many people became alarmed, and some hysterical when Orson Wells delivered the War of the Worlds over the radio. But, there was no question that those who did were the ones who actually heard it. No one was "hearing voices." It was actually in the air.

the false, and he knows the true. He is consecrated to its mission. He will assist all in its technology, theoretics, and theology.

Welcome, Space Visitors

It may be feared by many that if there is anything at all to what is herein alluded it would eventually penetrate to the potential enemy, forearm him accordingly.

In answer it can only be said that if the enemy should decipher the remote truths before we did, then fate wills the results that come to pass.

If there is nothing to this fantastic story, there is then nothing to worry about. If there is something material to it, then let us waste no time in silly speculation and questions.

There is no half-way measure here. It is either regarded as meaningless, or it is the fullness of knowledge and hopes allotted us to this day.

At present, the potential enemy is at least on a par with us in arms strength, so nothing is altered. Throughout history this situation has always been so.

If there is any substance herein contained, then it cannot be repressed, and the enemy may already have come upon it by the back door. There is no further argument; rather action ahead.

There are many detail courses of action which go in the developments, and there can be no rest toward the final ends.

It was actually in the air.

As for atmospheric phenomena it cannot be commented on here, for there is no atmospheric phenomenon, or aircraft that has ever behaved, or ever can, in the way the "flying saucers" can.

In time like these it would be even unpatriotic to see some unidentified object and not report it.

To report falsely with intention, or to dream up some hoax for ulterior purposes is for crackpots, and fringe criminals. In the greatest news in 19 centuries, however, these have been few in comparison with such that accompany o t h e r sensational news. Before long they will be virtually non-existent. All the hoaxers have regretted their antics. Little do they realize the majesty they are dealing with.

The Contact's Dilemma

There is no answer as yet to some questions that have perplexed even the contact subject. Perhaps they may be deciphered by others, or must wait the revelations of time.

Their actual names were never even alluded to. Their place of origin is a complete mystery as yet. The age of the visitors is not known. The maximum velocity of their ships in voyage can only be conjectured.

There was never anything but material reality in the contacts. However, the bottle of drink given Orfeo in the first meeting may have been an induced impression, as he did not hear anything when he dropped it. But

Page 7. Columns 1 & 2.

opments, and there can be no rest toward the final ends.

The future is either all delineated hereby, or one may choose to be inert to it forevermore. Nature reveals her secrets to the one and to the other alike. The good are favored, but they must be more actvie, also.

Calvacade of Progress

Space would not permit to recall all those whose keen perceptions and devotion to fundamental facts, and unique methods of investigation and discovery have added to the great edifice of modern science. It is interesting to note that the great significant era of science is divided into two periods. One being the era of basic discoveries and establishment of theories, which pulsated during the 19th Century, into the dawn of the 20th. The other period being the 20th Century, was more active in building up technical and mathematical static constants and laws, founded upon the former discoveries.

So great was the tendency to adhere to formulations, that basic knowledge and urges almost f a d e d completely. Technology now seemed to go by the law, the rod, and time, and the ETHER was merely in the way, obstructing many avenues and processes. Thus the ether has been nearly completely ignored, and even denied.

And also, fundamental progress has come to a near halt. For all basic progress was made from conception of the p e r v a d i n g ether. Man could use his imagina-

thing when he dropped it. But since the thirst and symptoms immediately had disappeared after he "drank its content," they must have released him from their instrumental control. Within the limits of physics, their capabilities appear to be magical indeed.

Was Orfeo himself visible from the outside when he sat in the crystal craft? He had no diffracting suit, but rather wore work clothes. This is another question not answered at the moment.

Orfeo will make no predictions, except to state what he believes will eventually evolve from inevitable events. What he sees for the future are not predictions, but expectations from the material realities of this world, and from the material realities shown him by another. The process cannot be accelerated. The impeding snag has been removed by the contact. For virtually three months he was a transformed human. That person exists no more. Within another three months he was his former self again, as though nothing had happened. But, he is today the most immutable convert on earth. He knows

ether. Man could use his imagination according to observing nature, and he hit upon hidden facts. The ether seemed to buoy their ideas to success.

Even today many have not abandoned the idea of the ether. But they would rather leave the case closed, and sink or swim with the main tide.

The case of the ether can never be closed. We can not just do with or without it, for it either exists or does not. With our indifference to it basic knowledge has almost ceased. **The ether is the only solid existent. All else are vacant entities as bubbles in its mass.** Proceed from there and all the unknowns of science give way to simple understanding.

This may all be looked upon as an elaborate yarn, one of many, that have accompanied the "flying saucers" phenomena, and is nothing more than an effort toward wordly gains.

Orfeo has turned his head on not one fortune alone, but on several. All were more normal, easier to persue, and more acceptable by the public at large. This effort can only bring sweat and ridicule from the very start.

if it were not exactly as written.

The real pearl is precipitated in an invironment of disease and corruption. The pearl alone survives; as truth has survived the hotbeds of adverse activities since time itself.

He could have contrived a yarn that the public would more easily digest, be financially rewarded, and be considered normal, even if a liar.

Some things are just not meant to be. Others were destined to occur in such a subtle manner that none could be aware of them at the time.

Time is the greatest testimonial of all. His affidavits are the Powers that be. His punishment for any deviation rests with them. Even to be chosen is punishable; but bearable. No one would care to face a punishment that would be beyond endurance.

The slightest contact between one world and another would surely result in opening the doors to the near ultimates of knowledge. This is done, and there is absolutely no alternative. The blue print for the future is within these pages. Feast on them, and develope them. They are as profound as all space; given from space.

We are visited by beings no more endowed than we. Only years advanced in time. They are fully aware of this.

Transparent, Yet Opaque

induced by some outside force. He merely kept to a corner, behaving as though he were singing. A song which he had never known before.

There was still another, occurring after he had decided to include these in postscript, and after the contact had been broken.

It was on the morning of October 16, 1952. At 4:30 he was awakened by a shrill hummnig, and high frequency vibrations which seemed to emerge from the metal bed springs themselves, and from the ceiling, so that he felt sandwiched in between two poles. This remained perfectly constant for twenty minutes, and was accompanied by a high frequency earth tremor. Both his wife and a neighbor young lady were aroused by this episode.

Six hours later Orfeo called the Seismological Laboratory, and they were glad to hear from him, for no one else had yet reported this particular tremor. Yet their instruments were picking it up at the exact time. Many days later the laboratory attributed its origin to the locality of Tehachapi, as residue tremors of the former ones. This could very well be. It is also definite, that the sound of the "flying discs" motion was for the first time to Orfeo audible. It was terrific beyond description. Perhaps there was a deliberate timing with the high frequency temblor.

Faith is a finer quality of the inner self. But from time to time

Transparent, Yet Opaque

Could it be possible that the craft in which he rode is so transparent that it is hardly visible, looking right through its entire structure? Yet, from the interior it is impossible to see even through a single thickness of its wall.

Of course the proposition sounds very improbable and unlikely. Orfeo can offer no explanation, but neither will he deviate from the statement. Fact or fancy it is thus presented, thus observed, and no conclusive explanation is possible at this writing.

Sightings and Contacts

He has seen, or deliberately been shown virtually every type of "flying saucer," and been materially contacted in various ways, and in revealing fashion. Yet much has been left to his imagination and mystification, as with everyone else.

Somehow, most certainly with highly processed instruments and devices, Orfeo feels they have been able to often merge his conscious forces with a degree of the sub-conscious forces. This phenomenon could account for a broadening of the intellect temporarily, and for the silent communion of one with another, with a minimum of oral talking. No one could have absorbed the fullness of the events unless the ones in control first "conditioned" the respondent.

inner self. But from time to time it must be nourished by at least even faint signs of a final fullfillment. Otherwise there is only a flashing existence, worthless.

In sickness it is good to have faith. But the appearance of the doctor is a sign that some help is at hand. If the doctor is good we shall not only be helped in some limit, but our faith is strengthened beyond doubt, no matter what the outcome.

Our space visitors are real. They are near perfection in a mortal sense. Look at them, depend upon them to do only what is right, and strive to be on the road to that goal. We need have no qualms about the future. But even beyond them, there is the Eternal. Who would be so narrow minded as to believe that the abilities and purposes of such an Infinite Intelligence could be limited or satisfied by creating an intelligent life on earth alone, an invisible speck in the limits even of our known universe? No, indeed. He is much, vastly greater than that.

Our efforts should be to leave the world as we would like to find it if we should return here. Prepare it for the meek and the infirm. After all, we do exist at this moment beyond any will or control of our own, and we cannot turn the course of nature. As long as life is felt and conscious, how can any of us cease to exist?

At all times life must be felt by someone. If only one person were left on earth, to each and

the respondent.

On Religion

As to the world's religious faiths, the visitors have never berated a single one. They have shown awareness and pleasure to the fact that Orfeo was God-conscious, and a Christian at heart. How they would have conducted with any different faith is not known.

Fantastics Omitted

In the text some incidences were omitted because they may be considered as completely impossible. Orfeo decided to include them herein, postscript, to make the narration complete.

One of these concerns the coin-like piece of "metal" on the floor of the craft as he sat there. This object was about the size of a silver dollar, and Orfeo knew it was meant for him to pick up, perhaps as a momento. The object seemed warm in his hand, and it felt active and "alive." It gradually diminished in size, and completely disappeared before he reached the ground again.

Another phenomenon was his "singing" while at work. It was not unusual to those who heard him. But on this particular instance it was totally involuntary.

Page 7. Columns 3 & 4.

were left on earth, to each and all it would seem that you were that one, no matter when or where. We are trapped, in His eternity.

Yet in all time we are allotted one awareness at a time.

20th CENTURY TIMES TESTIMONIALS?

The only testimony at Orfeo's command at the moment is time and this author. Time will reveal all. The author vouches for it without reservation. It could not be otherwise, for Orfeo and myself are one and the same. What occurred during those three months is like a phantastic memory, but as real as the ground we walk on.

Lie detector tests and such would be mere exhibitions, and would prove precisely nothing. Nature has never revealed anything rapidly, and we come to know divine order only after heart-rending efforts and much sweat. This is no exception. We cannot change it.

Yet we are ordained a testimonial far more impressive than any in the past. That is time, and we shall see these things come to pass in our lifetime. If the process were to be at random and rapid, they would land in our midst now. The issue is in other hands.

We have in these pages encom-passed the fundamentals of the incredible realties before us, from their structures, motive powers, capabilities, and their permanent presence. As we go on the entire universe will be shorn of many of its mysteries, hereih. What other testimonial could be ex-pected?

However, I do not know the in-tricacies of a universal order, the twists and turns of destiny. They may decide to land among us at any time, even though I do not believe it will be within hours.

If and when that should hap-pen, it is for all others. I would be denied and shunned at such a moment. It does not matter, for I would have little new to see or learn. Signs and realties are with us at all times. To those who discern "shall be given even more." Unfold; believe; discern, and see for yourself.

Orfeo Matthew Angelucci

To All plans and purposes the 20th CENTURY TIMES will be a regular monthly publication. Its policy is obvious enough. It will treat the real values of progress openly, and reveal the false or unreal to its limit. Once it assumes a problem it will not abandon it until some solution is reached.

In the forthcoming issues we shall present climaxes and anticlimaxes of this text, and include a chapter of Nature Of Infinite Entities for its full seven chapters, each month.

We shall see that free enterprise, and individual liberty are not dying, but that we have not even experienced them yet. All we have known to date has been either degres of slavery, or the survival of the fittest, with but token attempts at humane measures. Opportunities are not behind us; they are ahead.

Henceforth we shall appear as a magazine, at the popular price of 25 cents per copy. As soon as possible it will include one short story each issue, significant, world events, and interpretations of advances and discoveries to our best abilities. Whenever necessary our space visitors will command the limelight.

WE EARNESTLY WANT:

Writers of the future. Humane writers with blood in their systems. Writers with ideals, backed with realism.

We surely want contributions, but unfortunately cannot use insignificant or distorted material.

Letters expressing your opinions and sentiments are welcome.

Rates for basic material will be paid according to standards and respective values.

..Subscription getters will be paid a due commission, and we plan to give generous bonus to the ones sending in the greatest number of subscriptions. Details will be announced in subsequent editions.

Only bona fide advertising will be accepted.

We look forward to some day, perhaps soon, to become a weekly publication. Our children's future will be paramount in our ends. This is the publication America has long awaited for, and your subscriptions will underwrite it. Send it in NOW. Let us sever the chains that hold us, and unleash the tide of a new progress attested in the sky at every forward step.

Yours in service,

20TH CENTURY TIMES,

ORFEO ANGELUCCI, *Editor.*

IF YOU SEE ONE

If you see a strange object in the skies, would you report it? The Air Force is doing an excellent job, and seriously welcomes real sightings, in your best descriptions. We are both in unbelievable times, and in troubled times also. You and I must report anything that we know is not an airplane, balloon, or cloud, or any object which behaves in a truly strange manner.

Page 7. Column 5.

HORIZONS UNLIMITED

Recreation

Perhaps the oldest industry in the world is the newest, and remains constantly the newest. This is RECREATION. Perhaps the very first hours of man on this earth were spent in resting, and g a t h e r i n g his orienting senses. It seems that even creation continues only with the rythmic surgences of re-creation.

A few years ago there appeared in one of the major magazines an article titled "Recreation—America's Number 1 Industry."

There could be only one error found in that. It is truly the world's number one industry. past, present, and future. Everything that offers mankind a rest, a diversion, a pause of reflection and a moment of orientation is recreation. Even a job that one likes is a form of recreation.

Yet in this vast field we have remained as blind as a bat to its potentialities. For recreation is a thing spontaneous. It cannot be dictated to or corralled. It can be assisted but not controlled. In any resort spot on earth there is a complete expression of freedom both, on the part of the host and the guest. It is complete free enterprise and chance on the part of the host, and complete freedom of choice on the part of the guest. No other industry offers this boundless sense of free expression and movement.

Profit in Fun

We may feel that our future is in space and its conquest, and rightly so. But never was there a new land found, a new condition established, that meant the abandonment of the old. We still live in old lands, in same houses, and live by the same laws of nature. It is only our sense of values and visions that change, and give new value to the old. We may conquer space, and meet our neighbors there, but we must live

Our children, who are now learning what the past ha, learned, and who must explore the uncharted future do not want a slave state of conditions. They are hopeful, imaginative, realistic, dreamers. They are us all over again, with youth and ability to carry forward. We must hand the torch over to them, and it should be placed in their hand in full flame. Thus, we will know the satisfaction of knowing that our own visions and hopes shall become material.

Just to mention a few of the recreational fields to be fully entered into let us point to some, as follows:

BOATING — Develop unsinkable individual row boats. Revamp old sailing vessels, and build some new ones to sail into the seas for a few days to recapture the deep romance of the old sea life. Millions of people would patronize this repeatedly, to know th espell of the rolling seas and the swells, with another sail in the horizon as the sea wells up to meet the sky, and the defeated roar of a breaker on the prow.

RESORTS — We have hardly begun to awaken the public to the majestic lure of the deserts, to re-capture for many the Arabian Nights enchantment, which is more real today than ever before. Or the inner mystic, awesome atmosphere of the mountains, as they lie patiently waiting for us to awaken to their protecting hugeness.

Many more people could have summer or winter homes, even if they are only a one-room cabin to receive one in retreat at any time, whether in the country, the mountains, or the seashore.

MOVIES—Motion picture theaters and drive-ins will not die out tomorrow morning. People are company seekers by nature, and if the industry is well tackled by the powers that be, there will be a resurgence to the pay-in theater, and the popcorn and pop stand.

ARCHERY — This is perhaps man's most enduring and satisfying form of contest. Yet we have barely touched its potentials. We have concentrated on merely on darting an arrow into a nearby bulls eye. There is virtually no use of bow and arrow at moving targets, at distant shot placing, at shooting from horseback, and so on. These need promotive minds, with a lust for the genuine things.

Subscribe to
20th CENTURY
TIMES

LADIES' BILLIARDS — The games at billiards are one of the finest indoor sports. We do not mean the pool-hall gambling variety. We mean relaxing games of pool, which everyone can play with not too much exertion. Such lighter pastime is also a real boon to thousands who cannot enjoy more strenuous recreation.

There are literally hundreds of fields and new phases of the old. It is not enough to idly depend on things to develop, for nothing occurs without a motive force. The energies of the thinker and the doer must be focused along the right channels.

Chamber of Recreation

So free is the field of recreation, that there is hardly a body devoted to it, expansive as it truly is even today. Yet there could be created a "Chamber of Recreation," composed of leaders and various other members of the industry. There would be no control or governing strictly of the empire.

The efforts of this cooperative body would be to help develop the recreation industry, and to encourage the best elements into its folds. It would be their job to establish financial pools for use in private developments and loans. They would focus attention on places and phases waiting for exploitation and development.

This publication will devote part of its energies to the great industry of recreation in the future.

WE ACCEPT THE CHALLENGE

The whole universe teems with galaxies and stars and bodies, which are in constant motion at terrific speeds in our terms. They are all as "space ships" destined toward an incomprehensable journey. The evolutions contained therein cannot be deterred. Yet every detail is a challenge to every atom and every living thing contained.

On the human scene the 20th Century Times will endeavor to meet the challenge of all the negative forces as best it can. It considers the medical profession to be virtually the highest profession in our framework. That it requires censor at all is one of the negative and sad aspects of our society. But it is a challenge that we shall take up to the hilt, and there will be no let-up until the final way to correct the faults are to keep it free whereby we can also be free to give it a good going over. Once under state control it would become a monster, and even defy our housecleaning of its recesses.

We shall be active in bringing to light social injustices, and ways in which they may be erased. We intend to make every page alive with information and activity, from the better conceptions of the universe, to the slightest motion of a photon. Pictures and illustrations will fill generous amounts of our spaces. We plan to make you aware of the fact that we live in the 20TH CENTURY.

Page 8.

SAUCERS' FIRST REAL CONTACT REVEALED

From
WELCOME, SPACE VISITORS

The most amazing and INCREDIBLE narration of all time is here.
It is told in 8 brief pages of newspaper tabloid size.

In plain language, we are given the keys to the entire "flying saucer" phenomenon. There will be no material contacts, and any recent ones effected, except through this agency. Little technological progress can be expected except as given with this contact, and elaborated further in another article, "Nature Of Infinite Entities".

Included in the narrative are such as Avalanche In The Skies----We Are Surveyed----Their Search For A Contact----The Contact----An Attitude Is Changed----Opening Road----The Transformation----The Mission----Their Power And Motive Forces And Structures----

In postscript are included such as About Instant Disappearances--On Religion--An actual trip in space--our progress headed in their direction--testimonial--and other data.

During the sensational displays of 1952 an actual contact was executed.

For three months he was one of the "Space Visitors". It required three more months for him to become "normal" again. This was the author himself.

Every single person can be in contact from here on, but not he. He is spent and expended in a most unique mission.

Their future behavior, from the end of 1952, and ever after is well delineated.   All will be attested in the skies.

It is an EXTRA, in newspaper form of tabloid size, in eight pages, easy to read and fathom. But the paradox is as strange as the realities: none will believe, except in TOTAL.

By-   Orfeo Matthew Angelucci,   Publisher - author

Send for it now!
Twenty-five cents ONLY. (25¢)

20TH CENTURY TIMES
2931 Glendale Blvd.   Phone:
Los Angeles 39, Calif.   NOrmandy 3-3560

A brand new monthly.

Yearly --$2.50 in the United States and possessions.
       --$3.00 in Canada.